# STIRRING SPURS

---

## RAINBOW RANCH
### BOOK 1

## M.A. WARDELL

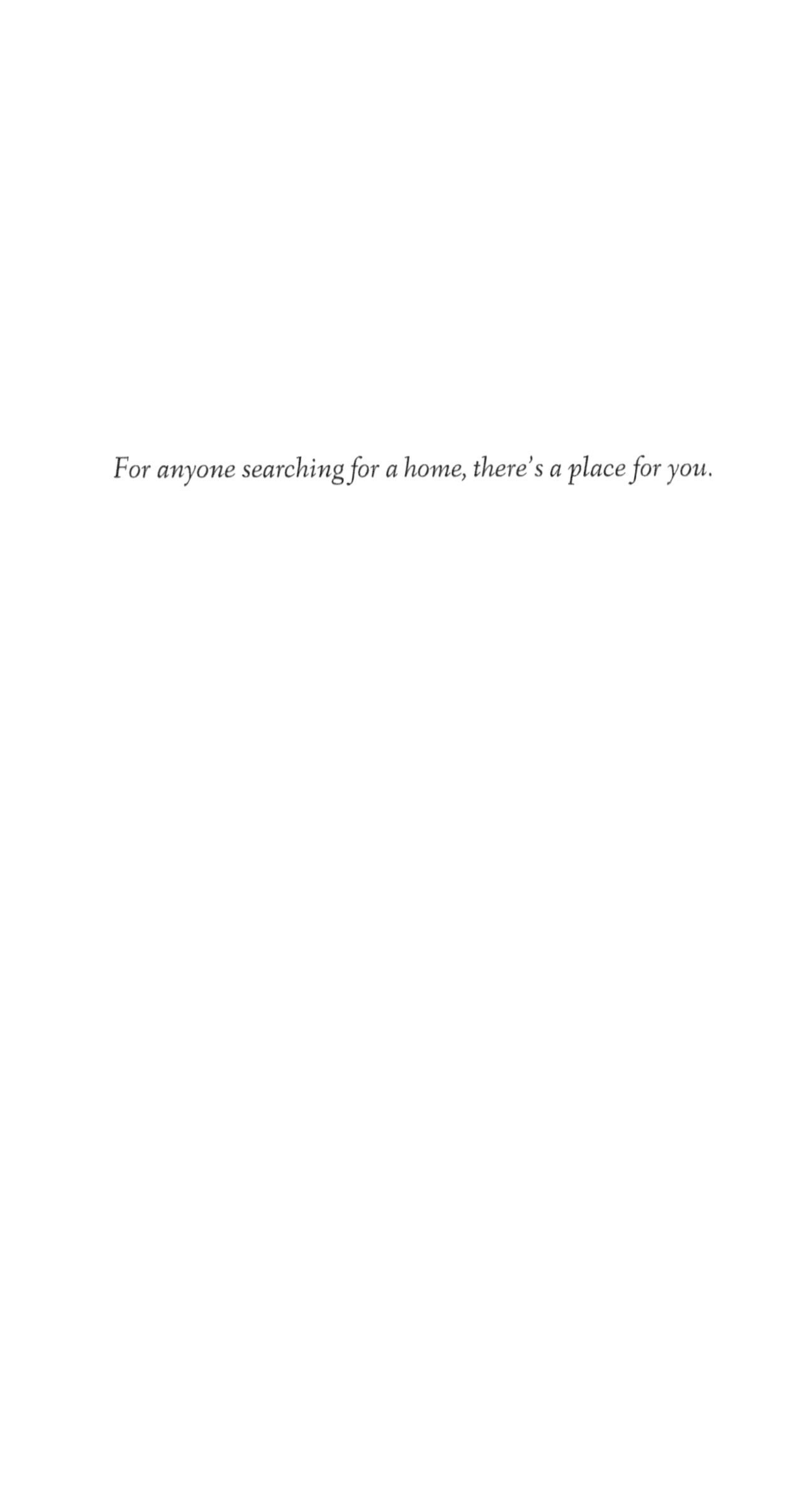

*For anyone searching for a home, there's a place for you.*

# AUTHOR'S NOTE

Dear Reader,

I'm honored to be the first entry in the Rainbow Ranch series. I cannot wait for readers to meet the Adams siblings and everyone on the ranch. Set against the backdrop of rural America, *Stirring Spurs* explores the rawness of human connection and the quiet power that comes from being true to yourself.

In writing this book, I wanted to create a space where queerness is the norm, where love between two men is simply a part of the landscape, just like the vast Oklahoma sky. In our world, there's still so much work to be done for queer voices to be heard and so much to unlearn when it comes to the systems that seek to silence or erase us. But on Rainbow Ranch, queerness isn't just accepted, it's celebrated. This queer-normative bubble offers a reminder: love is love, in all its complexity, joy, and tenderness.

Now, more than ever, we need spaces where our identities are not only acknowledged but woven into the fabric of our narratives. It's vital that we build these places, both in the pages of our stories and in the real world—these safe havens—where we can be free to exist and love as we are, without shame or fear. In doing so, we carve out a place where future generations can not only survive but thrive.

Thank you for joining me on this journey. I hope Boone and Wylie's story brings you comfort, joy, and a reminder that we all deserve to see our love stories reflected back to us.

All my best,
M.A. Wardell
(Matt)

*Stirring Spurs* is a sweet, low-angst story, but here are the content warnings if you need them:

Discussion of the death of family members before the story takes place, brief mentions of fatal heart attack, car accident, and alcohol abuse, mild internalized homophobia, as well as copious amounts of baked goods, chaotic mini-horse shenanigans, and dimple fucking.

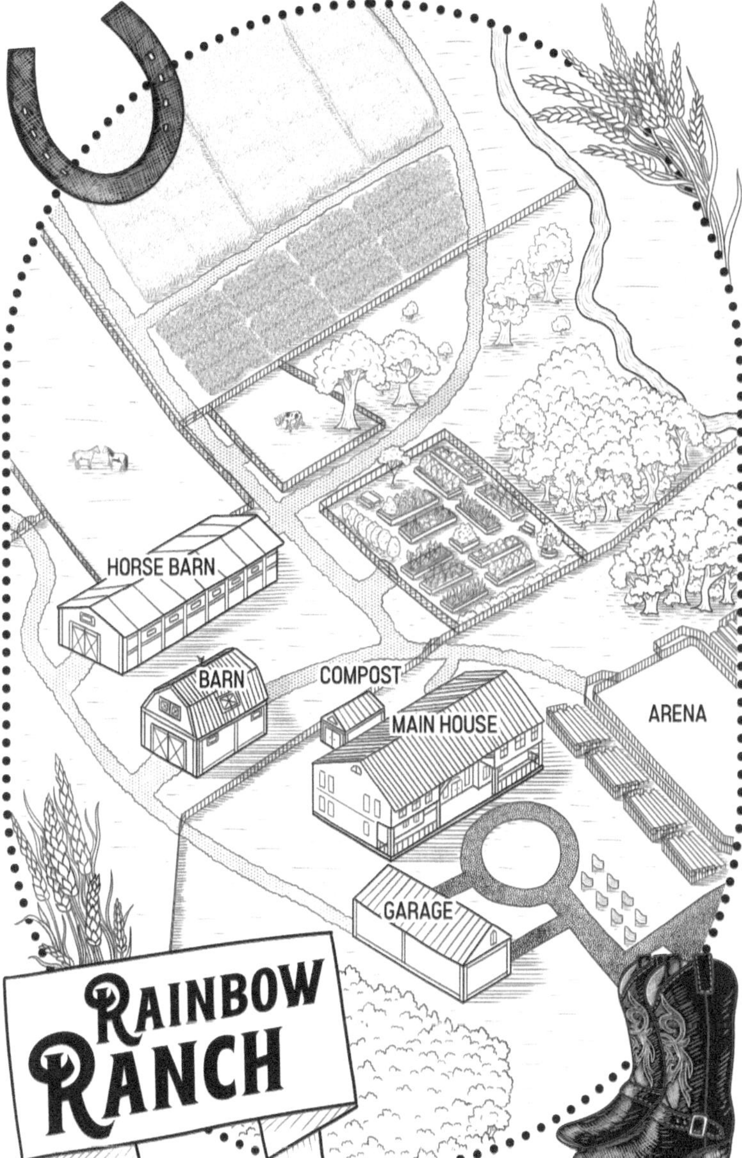

HORSE BARN
BARN
COMPOST
MAIN HOUSE
ARENA
GARAGE
RAINBOW RANCH

## BOONE

"SUNNY SIDE UP, COMING UP!"

Winnie smirks at my corny joke, sliding the carton of eggs towards me. The rhythmic crack of eggshells breaking against the aged cast iron pan, a sound as familiar as Ma's voice, signals the start of the day.

"It's always sunny side up with you. You do realize some folks prefer over easy. Some of us like our eggs cooked."

"Some of you are wrong," I say, grabbing one of Ma's old gingham dish towels so I don't burn myself on the handle. "Sunny always brings a smile to faces. And biscuits and rolls need something to sop up."

Winnie delivers an enormous eye roll and returns to icing the cinnamon buns. With her sandy blonde hair pulled into a ponytail and shoved under her Oklahoma City Thunder cap, she continues to work with a practiced ease, her fingers deftly finishing the buns as if she's done it a thousand times before. Because she has. The sweet aroma of sugar and orange rind competes with the sizzling eggs, and I glance at the armadillo clock on the wall. We often see armadillos 'round these parts of Oklahoma, and it adds a dose of much-needed whimsy to the kitchen's sparse decor. His little tail wags the seconds away, reminding me the table right outside the kitchen will be overtaken with chatter in less than five minutes.

I salt and pepper the eggs, the edges of the yolks starting to firm enough to spur me to grab the spatula.

"Almost ready."

I shake the pan, and even though I've crammed an entire dozen in, Ma's pan never lets me down. The eggs jiggle. No sticking.

"Work, Boone," Winnie calls. "Or make that, *werk!*"

As she teases me, I realize my ass has joined the party, shaking along with the eggs as a new country bop plays over the small radio in the corner. Holding a pastry bag of icing, Winnie joins me, swaying her hips to the music as I hum along. The clomping on the stairs signals a caravan of hungry mouths are en route.

As the chatter begins, I hand Winnie the towel and spatula, grab the freshly-iced buns from the counter, and head out to the table to greet my siblings.

We don't drive livestock on the ranch, but we still start early. Beau expects everyone to work by seven, so breakfast must be on the table by six thirty. At two minutes older, he's always been the de facto older brother. I'm two inches taller, his hair is longer, and he wears an elusive mask during rodeos to conjure up some mystery. Otherwise, we're identical. When strangers ask me what he looks like under the veil, I simply grin and point to my face. We may be twins, but Beau gives off major big brother energy, and after our parents passed, he naturally took the reins of the ranch.

"I smell orange."

Beau sits at the head of the long table. It's covered with a tablecloth featuring people on horses in various riding positions. As the ranch cook, my ass doesn't sit on a saddle, and I'm content to keep my distance from the beasts. Fresh pots of coffee, bacon, biscuits, and now my *signature* orange cinnamon buns blanket the table. Napkins and silverware are piled in the corner, and Beau passes them down.

"That would be the buns," I say, placing them within smelling distance of Beau's nose.

"We know you both adore buns," Billie quips.

She takes her spot next to Beau, her sleeveless black tank showcasing the intricate tattoo sleeves on both arms.

"Yes, Ms. Abilene, we do." I place a fat bun dripping with icing on her plate.

She shoots me her death stare, and for a split second, I see Ma in her eyes. Sure, Billie's hair is short, she probably weighs half what Ma did—and like her three brothers, she's queer—but she has Ma's nose. There's a tiny crinkle at the bridge when she smiles. I know she hates it when I use her full name, which is why I do it occasionally. We only have one sister, and Billie is tougher than all three of us together. Not needing any protection, as her brothers, it's our job to torment her.

"Three brothers, all homos. How did I get so..."

"Lucky," Benny intercepts.

"I was going to say cursed."

"You love it," Benny replies as I serve him a bun.

As the baby of the brood, we all take a little extra care watching over him.

"Winnie got a little overly enthusiastic with the icing on these buns, so this morning, I'm dishing them out." I hold the plate up. "Everyone gets one. Trust me, you want this cinnamon-orange sugar rush in your mouth."

"And we all know Billie likes sugar, ain't that right?" Beau teases.

"Don't fuck with me this morning," Billie says. "I've got to head into Johnson Springs for supplies, and I'm not looking forward to dealing with…"

"Hets?" Benny asks.

"People. But also, yes," Billie replies.

There's an unspoken understanding among the ranch staff that the first few minutes of breakfast are reserved for the Adams siblings. I place a bun on my plate and join them as Winnie carries Ma's old cast iron pan out and places it on a trivet. She lays the spatula next to the pan, winks at me, and heads back into the kitchen.

"Take Winnie." I nod toward her. "I can prep dinner by myself."

Winnie's a general hand on the ranch. And while she spends much time as my sous chef, she's at everyone's disposal.

"She peeled the potatoes for tonight's dinner yesterday, so I'm good. Take her. Let her be your buffer."

Billie's eyes sparkle. It's the same look she gave me when we were little, and I'd take her to pick wildflowers while everyone else worked. I don't care how old we get; she'll always be my baby sister.

"Are you sure?"

I nod and shout toward the kitchen, "Winnie, you're going into town with Billie."

"Awesome. Gets me away from your cheery ass for the day," she yells back.

"Why is everything about asses around here?" Beau asks. "We're trying to run a professional establishment."

"Because we're Rainbow Ranch." Benny smiles wide, showing his pearly whites.

"And we love ass," Billie adds with a smirk.

"Yeah, we do." Pris tightens the bow in the bandana around her neck as she joins the table.

As the head gardener, chicken wrangler, and manager of all things produce, Pris ensures the farm portion of our farm-to-table meals is intact.

"Speaking of butts..." I hand Pris a coffee. "How are those peaches looking?"

"Should be ready for your cobbler by the weekend." Pris takes the coffee and gives it a whiff.

"Well, now we have something to look forward to." Benny grabs a biscuit.

"If I have enough peaches, I'm making extra," I say. "Y'all seem to have a special fondness for it."

"You'll have more than enough." Pris serves herself two of the eggs, and I hear Winnie frying up more in the kitchen. "The trees are exploding with fruit this year."

"At least something's exploding," Billie glances at me, then Benny who proceeds to giggle.

"Excuse me."

"Just saying, glad something is... coming with gusto."

"Leave him be." Beau furrows his brows at Billie. "Not everything is about Boone's love life."

"Or lack of," Benny adds.

"Who has time for love when I've got this crew to feed? And speaking of, give me your plate, Pris. You need one of these buns."

"The only buns he's serving up." A smirk dots Billie's sentence.

Benny covers his presumably full mouth and laughs again at Billie's sass.

Pris hands me her plate, and I use a large fork to pry a bun loose and serve it.

"Hey, don't knock my buns." I place another fat bun on Billie's plate.

"Enough with the buns," Beau says. "We've got the new cowboy arriving this morning. He's going to take most of my attention today."

When our parents passed away almost seven years ago, Beau naturally became the head of the ranch. We quickly replaced the 'Adams' in our ranch name with 'Rainbow' and never looked back. It allows us to broadcast who we are and our priorities to the entire ranching community. Rainbow Ranch is a sanctuary that celebrates diversity, creativity, and community, combining the rustic charm of traditional ranch life with a progressive ethos. We welcome all orientations and identities here.

We've added some color to the ranch in the last few years. As you enter, a colorful array of flags flutter in the breeze, each representing the spectrum of queer identities. The main house, a cozy wooden structure our parents built before we were born, serves as our living quarters, but also a gathering place where we share stories and enjoy communal meals. From time to time, some ranch staff offer workshops that range from sustainable farming practices to artistic expression. Last year, Billie did a tattoo demonstration that brought folks from as far as Tulsa.

"I can help." Benny wipes at his mouth with a napkin. "Happy to take him on."

"I'm going to introduce him to Noodles," Beau says.

Silence takes over the table. Everyone turns their stares toward Beau, who continues to eat.

"Noodles?" Billie asks. "I thought we agreed he was a lost cause."

Our ranch is home to various animals—chickens, goats, even a few rescue dogs. For us, farming isn't just about crops. It's about cultivating a sense of belonging and nurturing relationships. We work to engage with the land and foster a deeper connection to the earth. Part of that is our livestock rehabilitation program. We take animals from challenging situations and put energy into helping them become active community members. It takes time, patience, and a lot of love. Sometimes it takes some fresh blood.

"No horse is ever a lost cause." Beau takes the last swig from his mug. "Some just take... more time."

"More time?" Billie asks. "It's been two years. He still won't let anyone saddle him."

"I'm not giving up on him." Beau places his napkin on his plate, and I take one last bite of my eggs, stand, and prepare to clear as everyone finishes. "Folks rode him before he came here, so he's got it in him. Somewhere."

Benny folds his napkin on his empty plate. "Let's see what this new guy's got."

As if on cue, the front door swings open with a sharp gust of air. A man wearing an oversized, wide-brimmed hat strides in. His broad shoulders fill the doorway, and heavy boots thud as he enters. He keeps his head down, and the shadow of his hat obscures his face completely.

"Well, speak of the devil." Beau stands to greet him.

The stranger lifts his head, and his deep brown eyes find mine. He's wearing a red and blue plaid shirt, unbuttoned to his sternum. Dark brown hair peeks out from his hat, and he stares at me with soulful eyes. There's a story there, waiting to be told. I grab onto the back of Beau's chair as my legs wobble under me. His rough exterior—a leather jacket and at least a few days of stubble—speaks of a man who's seen hard days and doesn't suffer fools. The sunlight streaming in from the bay window catches the fat round buckle on his belt. His face appears flat, mouth in a straight line, as Beau steps toward him.

"You must be Mr. Anderson. Come, sit. My brother will feed you."

## 2

### WYLIE

ENTERING THE HOUSE, I never expected to be greeted by a loaded table and the smell of freshly baked pastries. I'm used to beans, biscuits, maybe some scrambled eggs if I'm lucky. I haven't smelled anything so delicious in years, since I was a kid. My stomach churns, half-starved after the long walk from Johnson Springs. The inclination to hesitate hits me when I see the sea of faces staring up at me, and a grumble escapes under my breath as I peel off my jacket and look around the room.

Everyone's sitting and eating. I've clearly interrupted their breakfast. Except for one. A tall guy—at least a couple inches bigger than me—wearing a dark brown leather apron and matching hat, holds a plate of what I suspect is the culprit for the sweet orangey aroma permeating the room. He's criminally handsome. I pull my lips in and do my best to scowl. Of course, I'd happen onto a ranch with a hot cookie. Just my fucking luck.

He doesn't seem to notice my scowl as he holds the plate of golden, flaky buns out, practically glowing with warmth. He glances up, all sunshine and good cheer, not

9

intimidated in the slightest at the appearance of a gruff stranger standing in his dining room.

"Morning! I'm Boone. Have a seat. Let me fix you a plate."

He pulls an empty chair out, and I move toward it. The man who greeted me steps forward, places his arm around my shoulders, and introduces the crew.

"I'm Beau Adams. In case you didn't notice, Boone and I are twins." I take a quick study back and forth, and yeah, their faces are the same. Unlike his brother's hazel eyes, the cookie's are more green. Energy's all different, too. "And before you ask, I'm older. He's taller." I size him up—got a few inches on me too. "This is Billie, our sister, and the resident artist. Bennett, our baby brother…"

"Everyone calls me Benny."

I give him a nod and do my best to smile.

"He also works with the horses," Beau continues. "And Winnie helps with…"

"Everything." Winnie brings more freshly cooked eggs to the table and sits.

"That's Pris, the resident gardener."

"Nice to meet you," she says.

I nod and take my seat next to her. She's got the most beautiful black hair, like billowing clouds. She smiles, and I notice a few wisps of it poking out behind her ears.

Boone, the taller, younger-by-two-minutes twin, grabs a plate.

"Hungry, Mr. Anderson?"

"Please. Wylie."

The smile on his face hits me like a lightning strike. It could damn near melt frozen butter on a biscuit.

Before I can answer, he begins plating them.

"You look like you could use a little sweetness."

My brow furrows as my gaze flicks to the two enormous buns before me.

"They're not rattlesnakes," he says.

My stomach makes a noise, either from hunger or that damn way he's looking at me.

"Uh, I'm not really the sweet type," I mutter. "Just coffee."

He reaches for a mug and the carafe and begins pouring. "Sure thing. Cream?"

"Black."

Boone nods, a twinkle in his eye. "Well, you're in luck. Best coffee in a twenty mile radius."

"Only coffee," Benny clarifies, and Boone cocks his head at his brother. "But also, best."

Boone pours me a mug and hands it over.

"And if you change your mind, you might be surprised. My buns are famous around here."

Billie chokes on her toast as she laughs.

"My cinnamon orange buns," he clarifies.

My eyebrow raises as Boone hands me the cup of coffee. I take a sip—the bitterness hits first, but there's something smooth underneath like it might just take a minute to settle in.

"You're the cookie?" I ask.

"That's me!" Boone replies with a proud, playful grin. "Though I haven't been called that in a spell."

The guy smiles a lot. It's quite annoying.

"I'm pretty sure the universe can't function without breakfast. Have a bun. No one's ever died from a little sweetness."

I glare down at the rolls like they're about to start line dancing. After another sip of coffee, I set the mug down, and then—because these damn buns smell way too good—I pick one up.

"Don't mind my brother, Mr. Anderson," Billie says. "He just wants everyone fed and happy."

"Not sure it's my thing," I grumble, but I break off a small piece and set it on my plate before Boone opens those plump lips again.

My teeth sink into the warm, gooey icing, the intense citrus enveloping my senses, and when my mouth reaches the soft cinnamon sugary insides, my eyes narrow.

"...Huh," I mutter, trying hard not to smile. "That's not half bad."

Boone leans back against the wall, arms folded, watching me like a cat studying a mouse.

"Told you." He gives a soft, knowing look. "Tough guys need sweetness the most."

My head shakes, the rich, mouthwatering bun filling my mouth. When I finally swallow, I say, "You're trouble, aren't you?

Boone grins even wider, showing a hint of his teeth. "You've got no idea."

"Well, I guess Boone's buns really are beguiling." Billie licks the icing off her fingers.

Boone shrugs and winks at me. I almost drop my coffee, but I catch it. Fuck, no need to look clumsy in front of these folks right after meeting 'em.

"Where are you coming from?" Benny asks.

He's got a baby face, which tracks with him being the youngest of the clan.

"Broken Bow. Worked with some horses at the casino rodeo for a few months."

"And what brings you here?"

"Never stay anywhere too long. Don't want to wear out

my welcome. Heard you had some horses needing some extra attention."

"We do. And everyone's welcome at Rainbow Ranch," Beau says. "It's part of our manifesto."

"Literally." Billie points to a wooden carved sign on the wall that reads *Everyone Welcome*.

"Challenging horses are my specialty," I say. "I do my thing with them, then…"

"Leave." Boone, the cook with no business being that attractive, moves toward his sister's empty plate.

"Well, yeah. Do my job. And then, when I'm not needed anymore, move on."

"Makes sense." Beau wipes the corners of his mouth with his napkin. "Well, you're needed here."

Everyone at the table, clearly in on something I'm not, in unison says, "Noodles."

"Excuse me?" I ask, finishing the last of my coffee.

"Noodles," Beau repeats. "Finish your breakfast, and I'll introduce you."

"Need a warm-up?" Boone holds the carafe, and his face lights up like the stars in the night sky. Not exactly sure why he's so fucking excited about coffee.

"Sure, why not," I say. "It's the best damn coffee in the area, after all."

I shoot him a wink, and his lips curl into a smile. A dimple flashes, catching my eye. He might just be the most handsome man I've ever seen. Yup, definitely trouble.

---

"YOU CAME IN THAT WAY," Beau says, pointing down the main access road.

Dust still clings to my boots, and I recall the rumble of

the trucker's rig as it dropped me off miles back. Took me near two hours from the main road.

"But if you leave the main house from the kitchen," he continues, "you'll find the artery of dirt roads that lead to all the important places on the ranch."

I follow a half step behind him, doing my best to take it all in while he talks.

"Probably already noticed, but there's no cell service out here. Have to wait until you're closer to town to use one. We've got internet in my office and a landline you're welcome to use. Thought about getting one of those boosters, but we actually like the lack of connectivity. Forces us to be a little more present."

"Don't have a cell," I say with a shrug. "Job boards. Newspapers. Word of mouth. Maps. The world existed fine before 'em."

"Well, nothing to worry about then."

A cool spring breeze blows the large flags scattered around the property. We walk past the rodeo arena with even more banners flapping at the top of the bleachers, and I imagine it full of folks, watching and cheering.

"Sure do like flags, eh?"

"Pardon?" Beau stops in his tracks and turns to face me, and even only having just met him, I recognize the scowl on the bottom portion of his face.

"Flags." I nod toward a row of them surrounding the dirt arena, fluttering fast, making a thwapping sound.

"Oh. Yeah. We do. Started collecting them for the kids, but then they added so much to the property, we kept going."

"Kids?"

"The foster kids. Teens mostly. A few tweens, the younger ones. They come in a van from Johnson Springs on

Mondays, Wednesdays, and Thursdays. Rainbow Ranch helps them find their voice, feel at home, and connect with the land and each other. We hope to be part of giving them a fresh start. A few have stayed on after they've aged out of the system. Pris, the gardener you met at breakfast—she started in our teen program."

"Teens and animals. What can't you fix?" I ask.

"Ah, we don't fix anyone. Nobody's broken. Some just need a little more time and patience. We want to help. Isn't that why we're all here?"

"I mean, I guess. Sure," I say, but a tightness in my chest tingles.

This guy is full of crap.

I spot the larger barn in the distance. I'm guessing it can hold about twelve horses, or fewer if they're keeping other animals in the building. It appears solid and weathered against the sprawling landscape, its wooden beams faded by years of sun and rain. The roof, a patchwork of rusted tin shingles, slopes gently as dust swirls lightly around the foundation. As we approach, the wind whispers through dry grasses. The large doors of the barn are half closed, revealing shadowy interiors, and the faintest movement suggests the presence of its residents. My mouth curls into a smile when I hear a few soft snorts.

"Currently, we've only got ten horses, but there's room for twelve," Beau says, opening the doors fully. "Doc Evans, the vet in Johnson Springs, always lets us know of animals needing a home. We take in the strays, and he gives us a deal on vet care. We like to keep space for emergencies."

As we enter, the horses recognize their chances for attention, food, or both, and let out a few neighs. Beau grabs a bucket of apples hanging near a high window and feeds one to a beautiful mare.

"And they all ride in the rodeo?"

Even as the question exits my lips, I'm eyeing up some of these animals. They look healthy and well-cared for.

"Gosh no," Beau takes an apple from the bucket. "Only a handful. And the rest, we hope to include... in time. For now, we simply show them. Or not. We leave it up to the horses. Our rodeo is a little bit different."

My forehead crinkles. If I'm going to ride, make my cash, and vamoose, I need to get a grip on what I'm dealing with.

"How so?"

"Good boy," he says to a striking black gelding. "This is Jasper. He's Billie's horse. Or maybe I should say Billie is his human."

After only meeting Billie once, Jasper seems like the kind of horse she'd ride—powerful and majestic.

"Billie rides him in the monthly rodeo exhibition," he continues. "We shifted to calling it that a few years ago. Rodeos, in general, were getting a lot of heat, and for valid reasons. We aim to be a compassionate ranch. It's in our charter. We're here to rescue and rehabilitate, so our rodeos reflect that."

My head tilts as Beau talks, and Jasper sniffs at the apple in his palm.

"We prioritize animal welfare by altering the traditional events. Our goal is always to minimize stress and potential harm to animals and the riders. It's why we have fewer animals participating. By prioritizing the well-being of our animals over aggressive displays of dominance, we can maintain the spirit of a rodeo without jeopardizing our animals."

I shoot Beau a glance through squinted eyes.

"Yeah, yeah, I know." He leans in and softly kisses

Jasper's nose. "Trust me, I've heard it before—*the woke agenda has finally ruined rodeos*. But we find there are much bigger rewards this way. Because we treat our animals with respect, they thrive."

With my lips pulled in, I nod. When in Rome, and all that bullshit.

A tiny horse, barely up to my thigh, trots over, pushing at Beau's butt, and even though I try to stifle it, a laugh escapes. I've seen mini horses before, but never one *so* mini. He's dark brown with a few white patches that look like clouds scattered across his miniature body, and he's clearly in need of an apple or two.

"Okay, Dennis, okay."

Beau offers an apple, which Dennis snatches, crunches, and then proceeds to pace up and down the barn aisle.

"That's Dennis. Yep, named that because he's a menace. He's a mini, but don't let his size fool you—he's a total handful. A complete pill, really, always getting into mischief and causing a ruckus wherever he goes. Despite all his troublemaking, though, he's become the unofficial mascot of the ranch. Everyone here knows Dennis by name and adores him."

At the sound of his name, Dennis comes trotting over, kicking up a cloud of loose hay as he goes. With a playful snort, he makes a quick turn and bolts straight out the front door.

"Even if he's a little chaos warrior in disguise."

"Bet he's a hit at the rodeo," I say.

"Oh gosh, yeah." Beau's face cracks into a huge smile. Funny, he doesn't have the dimple like his brother. "He has a way of stealing the spotlight."

"So, your rodeos, there's no bull riding?"

Beau shakes his head.

"Steer wrestling?"

"Nope."

I clasp my hands under my chin. "Roping?"

"Breakaway only," Beau says with a shrug. "Nobody complains."

"Especially the calves," I reply.

This elicits a small chuckle from him.

I've seen breakaway roping at events, mostly with younger or female riders. The roper catches the calf but doesn't tie it. If that's what I gotta do to stick around and make some quick cash, so be it.

"Do you use spurs?"

"Don't typically need 'em," I say.

He gives a knowing nod, recognizing I'm a seasoned rider.

"Billie found some gentle ones we use when needed."

Whimpers and whinnies from a few other horses interrupt us as Beau pats Jasper's soft nose, and he chomps the apple.

"May I?" I ask, moving my hand forward.

"Of course." He rubs his fingers along the bridge of Jasper's nose. "He loves to be pet right here."

I follow his lead. With the horse under my touch, Beau takes the bucket of apples and begins feeding the other horses.

"Looks like Benny's already done the morning muck out before breakfast. He's up with the rooster."

"Does everyone take their meals together?" I move my hand away to follow Beau, but Jasper nudges my palm, and I return to petting his velvety muzzle.

"Boone demands it. Unless there are special reasons. Since our parents died, he's kind of become the mother hen." He looks up at me with hazel eyes. "Don't tell him I called him that. Ah, never mind, he'd probably love it. He takes care of us," Beau pats his stomach, "so we can take care of the ranch."

"And you guys are identical?"

They look alike, but brothers—twins or not—can be like that.

"He's two inches taller. His hair is shorter, but otherwise..." He moves his face toward me, giving me a good look, and yup, they're the spitting image of one another. "...identical."

Beau doesn't give me the same rocked-to-my-core feeling that his brother does. I guess it's not just looks, but something else. Something inside. Pop used to say folks have an energy, and I suppose looking the same would have nothing to do with that.

"He's a good egg, Boone. He'll make some guy very lucky."

*Guy.*

Heat rushes my neck at the thought of Boone Adams with a man.

"Is everyone here..." I hesitate, unsure of the right word.

"Queer?" Beau smiles. "Pretty much. We're open with the community. Damn, it's in our name—so we attract folks who want to work in an inclusive place."

When I first heard about Rainbow Ranch, I wasn't sure what to expect. I wondered if it had to do with colorful landscapes or if it had a connection to the queer community.

"And all four siblings? That's got to be some sort of record."

"Nah. Just sort of happened." He extends an apple to a smaller mare, whose lips curl and smack. She then nibbles and takes a big chomp. "And you..."

Don't talk about myself much like this, but Beau seems so open about it. I take a deep inhale through my nose and speak.

"Yeah. I mean... gay."

The word feels strange in my mouth. The moment it leaves my lips, I realize I don't think I've ever said it aloud. It's always been unspoken, leered at. But here, it seems as natural as the wind blowing.

"We accept everyone here. Every letter of the alphabet." He turns to me, eyeing me up and down. "If you ever get hungry during the day, head into the kitchen. Boone will take care of ya."

He winks, and my stomach gallops at the thought of his brother. Those thoughts can just mosey along.

Beau approaches the last stall where a large, blood bay gelding stands, head down. He's got a rich reddish-brown coat like a worn penny with a glossy black mane and tail. Even with his head lowered, there's no denying he's the most handsome horse I've ever seen.

"Now, this here is Noodles."

The horse snorts, nostrils flaring wide as he avoids Beau's hand, which holds a nearly rotten apple.

"Noodles?"

"Yeah, I know. Pepper, one of the teens, named him while cleaning his stall the day after he arrived. He arrived without a name, and they thought he needed something endearing."

"Okay, but Noodles?"

Beau shrugs and continues. "He came to the ranch from a bad hoarding situation outside of Stillwater. An older couple collected animals without the means to care for them properly. They had to euthanize quite a few, but we were able to rescue him. Billie, Benny, and I have all given him lots of attention to no avail. In a fit of frustration, I tried to ride him bareback last year, and landed ass up in the stream near the edge of our property. It took Billie and Benny the rest of the day to corral Noodles, and nobody's tried to ride him since."

Beau moves his hand toward the side of the horse's head, and he shudders, jostling back. "Right, Noodles?"

I recognize the fear in those giant black pools. It reverberates through the stall, and I wait for an opening.

"Would love to have him shown at the next rodeo."

"When's that?" I ask.

"Three weeks. First Saturday of the month."

I take a step closer. The sunlight from the window highlights his muscular frame, rippling with power beneath his beautiful coat. His mane and tail are long, wild, and untamed. His eyes tell a different story—wide, alert, and filled with deep, wary intelligence. There's a flicker of distrust in his dark orbs as if he's constantly calculating the safest distance to maintain.

"Be careful," Beau says. "Steady, boy."

I'm fairly certain he's talking to the horse, not me, but I proceed with caution.

Noodles stands with a slight tension in his body and a subtle arch in his neck. His large and strong hooves shift restlessly on the shavings, and given a chance, I'm sure he'd bolt. I take a half step closer, and his entire demeanor changes—his ears flatten slightly, and his gaze hardens, flicking back and forth as if deciding whether to flee or face me.

Noodles' nostrils flare, and his chest rises and falls with a quickened breath. He begins to shift back, but his hindquarters bump against the two-by-fours of the barn wall.

Without making eye contact, I kneel, bringing my head lower than his, and take my hat off. When he doesn't move, I lower my gaze to the ground and lift my free hand, palm outstretched.

The silence in the barn is palpable. The air escaping Noodles' nose mixes with the loud drumming from my chest. Beau remains still and quiet.

I inhale deeply through my nose and raise my palm slightly as I exhale through pursed lips. After another breath, the soft, smooth skin of the horse's nose makes contact with my skin.

"Well, I..." Beau whispers.

Keeping my palm steady, I rise slowly, settling my hat back onto my head as my other hand moves to gently support Noodles' chin, feeling the soft hair against my fingers.

"Good boy." I keep my voice low. "Good boy."

## 3

## BOONE

"NEW GUY IS... INTERESTING."

Winnie empties the smaller compost bin we keep on the counter into the oversized bin in the corner of the kitchen. The crackle of a breakfast's worth of eggshells cascading in accompanies the scratching sensation at the back of my throat.

"Weren't you going into town with Billie?" I grab a rag from under the sink.

"Change of plans. She needs to help Benny reshoe Jasper, and clearly, you need my help." She gives me a wide grin, showing all her teeth.

I roll my eyes but don't argue, happy to have her here.

"And as for Mr. Anderson—seen his kind before." I spray vinegar on the counters. "Coming through to make a few bucks, then moving on. We'll do our best to make his stay pleasant."

"Bet he could think of a few ways you could make his stay more pleasant," Winnie teases.

"Excuse me?"

"I saw how he was looking at you." She flicks the brim of my hat.

I run my rag across the granite I convinced Beau to install a few years ago. "Exactly how was he looking at me?"

"Like he'd been lost in the desert for days… and you were a giant pitcher of water."

Winnie's eyes widen, and she bursts into a loud laugh, filling the room with her joyous cackle.

"You hush. We're having French onion soup for dinner, and two bags of onions need peeling. That'll quiet your sass."

Winnie lifts the bags, one in each hand, and cocks her head.

"Boss, you know I've got eyes of steel. Challenge accepted."

We spend the rest of the morning cleaning and preparing for dinner. Since everyone's busy sprawled out over the ranch, we don't serve an official sit-down lunch. I prepare a small tray of sandwiches, fresh fruit, and a few paper bags of homemade chips and put them out after breakfast. They can grab 'em before they go or anytime during the day. This allows me to focus on tidying up, cooking dinner, and baking tasks requiring early prep. I'm lucky we're able to get most of what we need right here on the ranch. Between the gardens and animals, I can keep us fed with minimal trips to town for groceries. I'm still trying to get Billie to warm up to my homemade barbeque sauce, its smoky aroma battling the cloying sweetness of her preferred store-bought brand.

Winnie takes the onions out back to peel. Unlike her, my eyes will be a watery mess if she preps them in the kitchen. Left alone with the sweet country tunes sputtering from the radio, I make croutons with the sourdough loaf I baked yesterday morning. It's funny how day-old bread is the secret to crisp croutons. Sometimes, you need to let things get a little stale to truly appreciate them. Once they're in the oven, I'll make a couple fresh loaves for dipping.

"What's for lunch?" Billie grabs my waist from behind as I prepare the sheet pan for the bread.

"Peanut butter with peach jam or turkey with gravy."

"Hmmm. How am I supposed to choose between my childhood fav and an ode to Thanksgiving?" Her chin pokes my back and her slim, muscular arms squeeze my waist.

"Abilene Anne."

I turn around and pull her closer. I'm the only one allowed to call her by her full birth name and live to tell about it. When it comes to my little sister, I'm a total softy.

"Come."

I grab one of each sandwich, slice them in half, and put them together so she can have both.

Billie pushes a stray piece of bright blonde hair behind her ear. She keeps it short but is overdue for a trim. And then, in her final plea, she bats her eyelashes at me.

She may try to come off as tough as nails to the rest of the ranch, but with me, she'll always be the little girl I held hands with running in the fields chasing chickens.

"And these."

I retrieve my secret tin from the top shelf of the middle cabinet and pull out two of my molasses cookies.

"One for you and one for Jasper."

When I caught her giving my homemade cookies to her horse a few years ago, I started keeping a stash just for the two of them. Hey, big brothers are meant to spoil their little sisters—and their horses.

"Boonie."

She's the only one who calls me the nickname she came up with when she was a toddler—a name that's been with me most of my thirty-five years.

"You're the best. One from me..." she kisses my left cheek, "And one from Jasper."

With a peck on my right cheek, she takes the cookies and grabs a paper bag to pack her loot.

"Maybe some of your sweet charm will soften the new guy. He seems a little... cool."

Cool. Not in a flashy, all-show kinda way, but in shooing penguins from your feet kinda way. Ma used to say it all the time. *Don't be cool with me.*

"Maybe," I say, knowing she's entirely correct. "But Rainbow Ranch has a way of warming things up. Animals. Teens. Cool cowboys."

"Well, with how he looked at you, I think he might have some ideas on how you can warm him up."

"Not you, too."

"Excuse me." She places a clean cloth napkin in her bag and folds the top over.

"Winnie said the same thing." I nod toward the back door. "You two are pickled peas in a pod."

"No, we're just... observant. He was looking at you like..."

"Like what?"

"Like he's starving, and you're the first decent meal he's had in ages." She hip-checks me.

"Hush it," I say, snapping my dishtowel at her behind.

"Boonie, you haven't been with anyone in..."

She searches the ceiling and then begins putting her fingers up.

"I don't have enough fingers or toes. Winnie! Get in here. I need to borrow your digits."

As if she'd been waiting for a summons, Winnie's head pops in the back door.

"You rang?"

Winnie knows not to bring her onion-slathered hands inside my kitchen without washing at the spigot out back, but she's perfectly content to join the conversation from the door.

"When was the last time Boone was with someone?" Billie asks.

She's now sitting on the stool against the wall, making a triangle of the three of us.

"With someone as in..." Winnie starts.

"The biblical sense."

Billie makes an obscene gesture with her hands, indicating precisely what she means.

"You two are incorrigible."

"In-corra-what?" Winnie asks.

"Incorrigible. Awful."

"But you love us," Billie says with a smile.

"I do." I give her a peck on the cheek, her warm, spicy scent overtaking the distant onions.

Winnie moves so she's standing in the doorway, careful to keep her hands behind her back.

"And Billie's right, boss. You haven't been with anyone in a dog's age." Winnie scrunches her nose, either from the onions or trying to remember the last time I got lucky. "There was that time we spent the night in Johnson Springs, and you got your own room at the motel, but I didn't see you until we had lumpy oatmeal at the buffet the next morning. You seemed extra chipper. And it wasn't the breakfast. That was... three years ago?"

It was four years ago, but I'm not telling them that. Winnie and I drove into Johnson Springs for supplies—

flour, sugar, spices, parchment paper, oils, and extracts, the sort of things you can't easily grow or make on the ranch. We stopped at a cute little roadside diner and gorged ourselves on waffles made from a box mix, and when the busboy came to clear our table, he winked at me. When I went to the bathroom, he followed me and gave me his name and number. It had been so long, and we were away from the ranch. I splurged for Winnie to have her own room and texted Henry, who came after the diner closed. His name escaped my lips many times that night, but we didn't keep in touch after.

"I've got no time for boys."

I slice the sourdough into one-inch cubes with a long serrated knife. When the butt of the loaf is left, I hand it to Billie, who moves to the butter dish that lives on the counter.

"I'd say the new guy is more of a man."

She slathers the bread with the soft spread and returns to the stool.

"Whatever. I've got you all to keep in line."

I catch Winnie's eye roll in my peripheral vision.

"Boys. Men. They're trouble. All of 'em. Unless I'm feeding them, I have no interest. And they're typically not interested in me. Beau is the sexy one. His name literally means 'handsome' in French."

"Since when do you know French?"

"Since Julia," I say, grabbing *Mastering the Art of French Cooking* from the shelf where I store the cookbooks I rarely use anymore.

"You're identical twins. If he's sexy, you're sexy." Winnie tips her chin.

"He's got the whole brooding cowboy thing. I've got... an apron."

I brush my hands over the worn leather covering the front of my body.

"Brooding. Apron. It's all alluring." Winnie steps back and returns to peeling the onions a good two feet from the door.

"As your sister, I have no opinion on the desirability of my brothers, but it's fair to say you're both... attractive. I mean, you're my kin. You can't be all that bad."

Billie stands, the tattoos on her arms stretching as she flexes her muscles in an apparent show of our family appeal.

I reach for her, and she responds by wrapping her arms around me, trying to catch me in a headlock. Just as she's about to wrangle me into submission, the sound of boots stomping in from the dining room interrupts us.

Billie and I freeze, and Winnie gives her best shit-eating grin and glides away from the door.

It's Wylie—the new guy.

4

———

## WYLIE

"DON'T MEAN TO INTRUDE…"

The cookie and his sister are in some sort of skirmish, but their laughter tells me they're simply goofing around. Boone's trying to avoid what seems like Billie's attempt at a headlock, and his biceps flex under the tan flannel rolled up past his elbows.

"No, no, I was just leaving," Billie says, untangling herself from her brother.

"Beau said to grab lunch from you before we head out," I say, pulling my lips in.

Billie dips her chin and mutters, "Gentlemen," before sneaking outside.

Five seconds after she leaves, I hear her and Winnie giggling. Boone skips over and closes the back door with a loud thwap.

"Heading out?" he asks as he reaches behind me and grabs a brown bag from a shelf under the island.

"There's some fencing that needs repair. Near the outskirts. Beau mentioned a stream nearby."

"Oh, out by the Henderson's farm, where their property

meets ours. Yeah, that's a good few miles out. Beautiful ride. You'll be gone until dinner, at least."

He motions to a tray of food on the back counter. There are sandwiches, apples, and small paper bags.

"Help yourself. Take as much as you like. Nobody goes hungry here."

As Boone hands me the bag, his fingers brush mine, and immediately my face heats up, and my gaze drops to the floor. At a few inches shorter than him, I don't exactly feel dwarfed, but there's a subtle presence about him. He's wearing dark brown leather shoes that slip on easily, leaving the backs of his heels exposed. My eyes linger on his skin, aware of his gaze fixed on me.

"Much obliged," I mutter, hoping to grab my grub and get the fuck out of Dodge.

"Are you guys taking the truck or riding?"

Boone moves toward a large pantry near the back of the room and comes out with a small cooler that looks like it's been through a few rough adventures.

"Not sure. I mean, didn't say. B-b-beau," I stammer, and holy hell, I haven't stuttered since I was a boy.

What in tarnation is happening to me?

"Take this," he says, holding the cooler up. "I'm packing some water and tea. Unsweetened... since you don't care for sweets."

Boone smiles, and that tiny dimple teases on his left cheek. It's the first time I've seen him without his hat. His hair is much shorter than his brother's, but there's some length on top, and a single curl, which may be a bellwether for what it might look like longer, swoops down on his forehead. My fingers twitch, and I open my mouth to speak, but nothing comes out.

"Would you like me to throw in an extra sweet tea? Beau takes his sweet."

Again, my lips part, but the words get stuck in the back of my throat.

"Here's two. Plus unsweetened. Water. Toss your lunch in. I'm just going to make a bag for Beau. He'll forget, and he needs to eat, too."

Beau. Waiting in the barn. Boone's brother. Twin brother. Who looks so much like him, yet wholly different. Boone's got shorter hair. That curl dripping down his forehead like molasses. Those bright green eyes. The dimple.

"Beau."

The word slips out, and Boone raises his eyebrows and grins.

I'm a complete gutter snake.

"Your brother."

"Yes, I'm aware. Shared the womb for nine months and all."

He pulls his lips and exposes his teeth, the dimple doubling in size as my stomach flips. I reach for the cooler, and again, Boone's fingers graze mine, but I keep my head up this time. My brain sends the signal to my face to smile, but I can tell nothing's happening—stone cold.

"Let me just pack a bag for Beau," Boone says, placing two sandwiches and three apples into a rustling brown paper.

"Three apples, eh?" I ask, and now the full smile appears, happy with my question.

"For the horses. If you take the truck, save 'em for when you return."

"Got it. Yes, sir."

Sir? What in the devil is wrong with me?

"Boone's fine." He smiles, and my nerves calm a bit. "No need to be formal."

He places Beau's lunch into the cooler and then puts another small brown bag inside before closing the lid as I hold it.

"A treat. For Beau. I know you don't fancy sweets, but maybe he'll share if you're nice."

We're no more than a foot apart, and warmth creeps up from my toes and scurries up my boots to my groin. I turn to go, but Boone's hand lands on mine, gripping the handle.

"And Wylie." He's taken a step closer, and I spot the flour dusting his shirt and apron. "I don't bite."

My eyes widen, and a boulder-sized lump appears in my throat.

He winks, and the creeping warmth transforms into a flash fire, consuming my entire body with heat. I yank the cooler away, the rough plastic scratching against my hand, and sprint toward the front door faster than I've moved in ages.

---

DRIVING along the ranch's open fields in what appears to be a fairly new Dodge Ram, I can't help but admire the polished chrome accents in the cabin as the engine purrs. The truck handles the terrain with ease, its tires gripping the ground as the wind whips against my arm hanging out the window. We're so high up, yet somehow grounded and invincible.

The sun shines brightly in the sky. There are a few clouds, but they don't put a damper on the warmth. The hum of the pickup's engine underscores the ride as the ranch slowly unfolds—vast, rolling fields dotted with cattle grazing lazily. As we drive, a few outbuildings starkly contrast their surroundings. They're all painted bright colors of the rainbow. The smell of the earth and fresh hay drifts through the open windows as the truck's tires kick up dust, and I can't help but feel a quiet connection to this vast, untamed space.

"We'll have to work Noodles up to riding." Beau stares out the window. "I was told he was ridden before, so he can do it. Just doesn't seem to want to anymore."

I nod, momentarily glancing at my palm, where the horse made contact a few hours ago.

"Sometimes all they need is the right person," Beau says. "Maybe that's what brought you here."

I shrug. "Maybe. He'll be ready soon. I can tell."

"After just meeting him? You weren't here when he threw me over the fence. He's going to take a slow hand. You could have ridden a different horse today. Kayla is a beauty, and she'd let a donkey on her back."

I shake my head.

"Nah, better to wait."

Don't want him thinking I'm odd, but I don't want Noodles seeing me on another horse until we're further along. Until we've built a stronger connection, no need distracting him.

"With all this gear..." He juts his head out the quarter glass. "It's for the best. Plus, that cooler Boone packed us is stuffed to the gills."

The mention of his brother's name sends goosebumps trotting over my arms. I haven't stammered like that since I was a kid. Back then, the special teacher at school helped me work through it—or at least, I thought she did. That damn cookie has me all flustered. My mouth goes dry thinking about him, and I have to work up enough saliva in my mouth to speak.

"He packed you two sandwiches. Three apples. A bunch of water and tea. Then a bag of some sweets, but he didn't say what. He's sure..."

"Handsome?" Beau finishes before I can.

"Was gonna say a ballbuster."

"But also, handsome, right? I know we share the same face, but objectively, it's handsome, right?"

Blood rushes to my head, and a fire blazes across my cheeks.

"Wylie, if you're going to stay with us on the ranch for even a few weeks, I just want to make one thing clear."

His tone is a mix of protectiveness and sincerity as I look over and see that he's staring out the front windshield.

"I love my brother more than anything—he's my best friend, my family, the one person who's always been there for me. But he's also got a way of focusing so much on all of us, he forgets about himself. He's got a heart of pure gold—loving and kind to everyone. He'd give you the shirt off his back. Which would leave him half naked." He wiggles his eyebrows. "Please be careful with him."

I just arrived at the ranch this morning, and I'm already being lectured about being careful with the cookie's heart. Was my tongue hanging out of my mouth like some kinda fool at breakfast?

Then again, I can't argue with anything Beau's said. This is his twin brother. They share a connection I'm unable to fully understand. And he sensed something.

"Did he say something to you? About me?"

He huffs. "Gosh, no. Didn't have to. I know my brother. He's only made eyes like that for one other person, which didn't end well."

My heart trips in my chest, thinking about Boone with someone else.

"Anyway, I'm not trying to scare you. Just know we're a family ranch, and Boone is a central part of that family. Treat him well, and we'll have no issues."

We continue driving, silence taking over the cab as a cloud of dust trails the truck.

Family. The Adams brood seems to be tighter than a litter of pigs in a barrel. My head swims with memories of my brothers. My parents. We never had much, but we had each other, and that was always enough. Pop, a grizzled rancher with worn hands and a heart of steel, taught me the value of hard work before I could even walk. Maw, a quiet woman with a gentle smile, filled our home with warmth. My brothers, Luke and Jesse, and I were only separated by a few years. Maw used to call us the Three Amigos, always causing mischief. We were inseparable, working the ranch, laughing, and living a life that seemed as steady and certain as the wide Wyoming skies above us.

But everything changed that distant, bitter winter night when a snowstorm rolled in faster than anyone could have predicted.

"Over there." Beau's voice pierces the silence, bringing me back. He nods over to the left.

The truck rumbles on the dirt road, which seems to have been created by its tires, and a fence lies fractured ahead. Broken, splintered wood sprawls across the ground like a half-finished puzzle. We slow to a crawl, the engine's hum fading as I take it in. A few posts are still standing, but the rest have been knocked down, the remnants of something the earth once held together. It seems recent—like trouble came calling, and the fence gave way.

Beau stops the truck, opens his door, and says, "Well, fence won't fix itself. Let's do this."

5

———

BOONE

WITH EMPTY DESSERT plates scattered around the table, I take a seat next to Benny, the lone member of the ranch who hasn't fled for either the bonfire, a card game, or the privacy of their room.

"Fantastic dinner," Benny says. "As usual."

"Well, I'm glad you enjoyed it."

He licks the last of the icing from his fork, and holds it up like a trophy.

"Best damn cake. Ma would be proud."

The corner of my mouth twirls into a grin thinking about her.

"She always said don't mess with simple. A sheet cake will make everyone happy."

"And she was right." He licks the last of the strawberry frosting off his fork and stands.

Without getting up, I lean over and begin gathering the empty plates.

"Want me to help clear?"

"Nah. I managed before Winnie, and I can manage on her nights off."

As a general ranch hand, Winnie is pulled in every direction and typically works from sunrise to bedtime. She gets a full twenty-four hour break every four days, and her break started this afternoon. When Pepper, one of the teens, is here on Winnie's day off, she likes to help in the kitchen.

"Boone-dog, listen. Your family is allowed to lend a hand. Just ask. Or accept if we offer."

"You've been outside with the horses all day. I'm good. I promise."

I lean over and plant a kiss on his shoulder, the worn, musty flannel of his shirt a sign the boy needs to shower and do laundry. But even if he's my baby brother, he's not a kid anymore, so I keep my trap shut. Might just do a load for him, though.

The thud of boots on the wood floor that lines the hallway into the dining room causes both Benny and I to pause our conversation as Beau and Wylie walk in, hanging their hats on antique hooks along the wall.

I stand, cock my head, and put on my best impression of Ma's annoyed look. When I open my mouth to speak, Beau intercepts me.

"I know, I know, Boone. Early is on time, on time is late, and late is unacceptable. But besides the fence being knocked down, turns out there were structural issues I didn't foresee. A few of the posts were rotted out, which is probably why the section collapsed in the first place. We needed more lumber than I'd planned for, which meant we had to head into town. The whole thing was a cluster."

I do my best to keep my face frozen, but Beau knows me too well.

"I've already put all the leftovers away."

"Oh. Well, we can fix our own plates," Beau teases.

"You'll do no such thing. The soup needs the cheese

melted at the last minute. And the croutons need a quick warm up so they're not soggy. I'll throw your dinners in the oven while I get the soup ready."

Beau walks over, wraps his arms around me, and gives me a squeeze. Having a twin means a unique bond that goes beyond shared experiences. There's an unspoken connection that often makes communication effortless. Beau understands me in a way nobody else does. He knew I was gay before I did. When I came out to him at fourteen, he simply hugged me and said, "Thanks for finally telling me." Six months later, he told me he was pretty sure he was queer, too, but not gay. "I think I just like everyone," he said. Wasn't sure it was possible, but somehow it brought us even closer. Pa used to say, "Beau and Boone, like butter and biscuits."

"Soup's on," I say, returning from the kitchen with two steaming crocks. "Give me five minutes, and I'll have your dinners."

"Listen, Boone, I know it's against house rules, but I lost a good few hours on the fence today, and the paperwork and bills aren't going to take care of themselves." Beau stands, reaching for his soup. "Need to call Doc Evans about a few things, too. I'm going to take mine to the office and get caught up."

He shoots Wylie a quick wink, not even trying to conceal it from me.

"But your dinner," I say, turning toward the kitchen. "Don't move."

I grab a dish rag and fling the oven open, retrieving one of the plates I'd made up earlier and return to the table.

"You take the soup," I tell Beau. "Mr. Anderson, please eat."

As we head down the hallway, Beau turns to Wylie,

plants a smirk on his face, and says, "My brother will be right back."

I accompany Beau into the office near the front of the ranch. A small and rustic space, it's simple but organized. Paperwork and notebooks blanket his desk, but he's managed to make piles to try and wrangle the chaos. The ranch landline, an old, yellow phone that's been here as long as any of us can remember, sits on the edge of the worn wood. There's a laptop nobody but Beau really uses and a small wood stove sits in the corner, waiting for colder months.

He sits with his soup, and I place the plate next to the computer on the desk and carefully close the door.

"Beau Bently Adams, what are you up to?"

"Oh, my full name." With an amused look on his face, he arches an eyebrow.

"Nothing," he says, lifting his hands. "I swear. I need to get these bills paid."

He points to the wooden mail holder on the corner of the desk.

"Plus check email. Get the payroll ready for next week."

"You could take twenty minutes to eat at the table."

"I mean, I could." There's a gleam in his eye I know all too well. "As your older brother, I'm asking you—please. Go. Keep Mr. Anderson company."

"Two minutes older," I say.

"Worst two minutes of my life." Beau takes the spoon and pokes at the melted cheese covering his soup. "Waiting on your ass to arrive."

I shake my head, turn, and head for the door. Before I open it, Beau says, "Love you more than a rodeo ride."

"Love you more than the sky wide."

I can't be mad or annoyed with that face for long, and

Beau knows it. It's literally my face. Walking back to the dining room, I get my first good look at Wylie without his hat. His hair is longer than I thought. It's wavy and damp, probably from working in the sun all day.

He yanks the spoon out of his mouth. "What in tarnation?"

"Something wrong? Do you need salt? I try not to add too much. She wouldn't want me to spill her tea, but Billie's watching her blood pressure, so I go easy on the salt. Let me get you the shaker."

I fetch it from the hutch on the wall and place it next to him.

"No. Sir. This soup…" He nods at his bowl. "Better than a cool breeze on a hot day. I've never had grub like this. At ranches it's usually burgers. Beans. Chips. That sort of thing. Not used to a cookie like you."

"Oh. Well, we do things a little different here. Ma always said the better the food on the plates, the better the work on the ranch."

"I haven't eaten like this in… well, a really long time."

He takes another bite, the melted Swiss leaving strings on his chin as he brings the spoon to his mouth.

"You've got a little," I say, handing him a fresh napkin.

"Gosh, look at me." He wipes his face. "Can't take me anywhere."

"You're good." I'm struck by how sweet he looks with cheese stuck in his stubble. "French onion is a favorite around here, but it's awfully messy. Let me get your dinner plate."

Returning from the kitchen with two plates, I sit next to him, and place a fork and knife on both our napkins.

"You haven't eaten yet?"

"I had my soup with everyone earlier, but without

Winnie, I was too busy to sit for dinner. I made myself a plate along with you and Beau."

"You made all this?" He pulls his plate closer.

"Sure did. And everything on your plate comes from the ranch. Pris and I coordinate crops with menus. There was an abundance of zucchini so I whipped up some ratatouille. Our potatoes are some of the best in the state. I didn't have as much time, so I roasted them in the oven while the veggies cooked."

"Well, this sure beats beans on toast."

"Thank you. I appreciate that. It's nice to have a new mouth to stuff."

Wylie coughs and covers his mouth with a napkin, and I grab the pitcher of water to fill his glass.

"I just meant everyone around here's used to the food. So I'm grateful when someone new comes along."

He nods and takes a bite of chicken.

"Lord. This sauce. It's... sweet. Tangy. A little heat on the backend."

My face cracks into an enormous smile.

"Ma's recipe. Want to know the secret?" I ask, leaning toward him.

"Sure."

"If you tell anyone, I'll have to tie you up and tickle you."

His eyes go wide.

"That's what Ma used to say to us kids." I wink at him, his dark brown eyes going even wider. "Anyway, there's coffee in there. And a little bit of peach puree."

He shakes his head. "Ain't that somethin'? Coffee and peaches in barbeque sauce. Who would've guessed?"

"Remember, it's a secret," I say, and mime zipping my mouth shut. "No telling."

"Who would I tell? The horses?"

"Well, don't. Unless you fancy being tied up." I shoot him a wink, and this time when he lowers his head, there's no hat to veil his face, and I'm able to witness his cheeks flush pink.

"How'd you get to be such an amazing cook?"

"It's all Benny's fault."

"Your brother?"

"Yup. With seven years between us, Beau and I were already helping our parents with chores around the ranch by the time Benny was born. His birth and infancy is what pushed Ma to let me help more in the kitchen. Beau was always outside with Pa, and I stayed in the kitchen with Ma. I went from sitting on the stool, gathering ingredients, and cleaning up after her to being her hands while she instructed me from the rocker Pa moved into the corner of the kitchen." Mr. Anderson takes a long draw from his water, and I move to fill it back up. "By the time Benny was walking, I was able to make almost anything Ma could without her guidance. For the next twelve years, Ma and I worked side-by-side. As she got older and standing longer and using her hands became more difficult, I slowly took over."

"Imagine if he'd never been born. You might still be sitting on the stool in the kitchen."

"I suppose," I take a sip of water and attempt to fathom a world without Benny under foot or me in the kitchen.

"Now finish up so we can have dessert." I put my fork down and wipe my lips. "Oh wait, you don't like sweets."

"I mean, depends on what it is." His lips ease into a half smile. "And my mood."

I stand and retrieve the plate covered with a large upside down roasting pan and place it on the table before us. Lifting the pan, I reveal the vanilla sheet cake slathered in my homemade strawberry buttercream frosting.

"Cake?" Wylie takes the last bite of his dinner and pushes the plate to the side.

"Sheet cake—nothing fancy, but why mess with..."

"Simple," he says.

"Exactly. The classics are classic for a reason. Everyone loves cake. What do you think, Mr. Anderson? Fancy a slice?"

I hold the spatula, ready to serve.

With his lips pressed into a line, he glances at the cake, then me, then back to the dessert.

"Sure. I mean, pretty sure it's a sin not to have cake."

"I couldn't agree more. Here's a corner piece. Extra frosting. Just leave whatever you don't want."

I place a dessert fork next to his plate, but instead of digging in, he lifts the cake to his nose, taking a deep inhale.

"Smells like..." He closes his eyes, and when he takes another sniff, a tiny dab of frosting lands on his nose. "Heaven."

"Um, you've got a little... just... Here, let me."

I reach over, swipe the frosting from his nose with my index finger, and pop it into my mouth.

"Delicious." He gazes at me as if I'm sweeter than the cake itself.

"You haven't tasted it yet." I nod to the plate.

He nods and takes a large forkful into his mouth. His face melts like a marshmallow over a campfire. Ma was right. There's a direct path between a person's heart and stomach.

"Mmmmh. Damn that's good as gold."

We sit and eat our cake, swapping an occasional smile when he moans with pleasure at the simplicity of vanilla cake with strawberry frosting. It's hard to ignore the scruff that covers his severe jaw as he chews. When a dollop of frosting finds its way onto his lip again, the sweet, sugary scent fills the air before he wipes it off with his napkin, leaving me wanting another taste. But I'm left watching as I eat my piece next to him.

Wylie clears his throat, the sound heavy in the still air. "Guess I should get to bed. Got an early morning." He folds his napkin with a sharp motion and sets it beside his plate. "Need me to help with the table?"

"No, sir," I say, "But hold on one sec."

I retrieve a paper plate, plastic fork, and roll of foil from the hutch.

"Let me give you an extra piece. You know, in case you wake up in the middle of the night craving something sweet."

"You don't have to do that," he says, grabbing his hat from the hook.

"Of course I don't. But now I know you like... certain sweets."

The foil crinkles as I tuck it under the plate and hand it to him. Our fingers brush again as he takes it, and a spark flickers in my belly—like the sudden flare when I light the stove.

"Much obliged."

With a slow, deliberate motion, he tilts his head back, his eyes locking onto mine for a heartbeat. One corner of his mouth turns up in the slightest hint of a smile, and he heads toward the stairs. As I watch him walk away—his jeans hugging everything just right—I catch the faintest taste of frosting on my lips. Unable to resist, I run my tongue over my mouth as my eyes focus on Mr. Anderson's ass.

## 6

## WYLIE

AFTER WASHING up in one of the shared bathrooms in the hallway, I return to my small room, my eyes closing as the door clicks shut, and I throw the small lock over the knob. A single bed sits in the corner with a small table next to it. A tall, narrow dresser and a little wooden chair rest on the opposite wall. That's it. Sparse and simple, but it's all I need. I won't be here terribly long, and for now, I'm leaving my clothes on the floor in my old duffel. No sense getting too comfortable.

Never thought I'd leave Wyoming, let alone my folks' homestead. But here I am. Ten years gone. Thirty-four years old, and not really sure where I'm going or what I'm looking for—just gotta keep moving. Stay anywhere too long, and you plant seeds. Nothing good ever comes from seeds taking root.

It wasn't the only reason I left, but it sure as hell played a part. For as long as I can remember, I've known something about me was different. Not like my brothers, not like my old man, and certainly not like any of the other men we had around the ranch or in town. Tried to shove it down for as long as I could, but it never quite stayed buried. Pretty sure my family knew, but never said anything. I never took an interest in women the way Luke and Jesse did. We were busy working—who had time for anything else?

The truth? I knew full well that the kind of love I was after was never gonna fly in a place like that. A town like ours? They wouldn't get it, and I sure as fuck wasn't gonna stick around to be someone's lesson in tolerance. It's gnawed at me ever since—riding from one place to the next, trying to outrun all that mess.

Years on the move, and I end up here, in a place where no one knows my sad story. With their brightly painted buildings and every queer flag in creation flapping in the breeze. And the best part? Nobody gives a crap who I fall for. Especially not that chipper cookie with the damn dimple in his cheek. Maybe that's what I need—something new, something I don't have to drag around with me like a millstone. A fresh start. Maybe a few weeks on Rainbow Ranch will do me some good. And hell, if nothing else, with all his fancy cooking, I'll leave a few pounds heavier.

I hang my hat on a hook behind the bedroom door, sit on the edge of the bed, and kick off my boots. A blister on my right big toe bubbles under my sock, and I wince as the pressure of being crammed into leather all day releases. I lean back on the thin mattress, and the coils of the bed squeak as my head rests on the flimsy pillow. My eyes shift to the moon and stars out the window beside the bed. The shade is up, but being on the third floor of the ranch, I leave it. Nobody but owls and bats looking in. Maybe I'll give 'em a show.

I unbutton my shirt and peel off my tank. My fingers graze my chest, getting lost in the hair. Unlike my brothers, who never grew much anywhere but their heads, mine's covered in a soft, thick layer. The few times I've been with men, they've seemed to appreciate it. Burying their fingers. Faces. Tongues. Fuck.

The tightness in my jeans becomes uncomfortable as Boone's face swims in my head. That smile. Those damn green eyes staring at me as I ate his sweet cake. I reach down and unbutton my fly, and my dick immediately springs to life. Quickly, I stand and strip, the moonlight catching my face as I pull the patchwork blanket back and return to bed. With another glance out the window, I spot a figure moving in the distance. As a reflex, my hand covers myself as I squint and try to figure out who's out so late.

Near a purple rustic outbuilding, about a hundred feet from the main house—Beau said it was for storage, trash, recycling, and composting—the image comes into focus as my eyes adjust to the darkness.

A bright light clicks on—one of those fancy motion detector ones—and I see him. The cookie. Boone. He's kneeling, bent over. His body shakes, and I quickly realize he's emptying something. Garbage. Food. Scraps. As my eyes screw up to make out the details, my thumb grazes the head of my cock. And yeah, he's so fucking far away—he'll never know.

I scoot closer to the window, my legs apart, my face resting against the smooth, cool wood of the window casing as my fingers warm from gripping the heat of my dick. He's got a few containers. There's a wagon or cart of some sort next to him, and as he empties each one, he returns it and grabs another. Who'd ever think Boone Adams bent over bins would give me such a raging boner? Probably not him.

He had to be flirting with me. The icing. And cake. And all the talk of needing something sweet. What would he think if he knew I was staring at his round ass in those tight jeans as he wiggles to get every bit of trash loose? Fuck, I'd like to loosen him up. Cram my tongue up there first to get him nice and ready. Slick. Glide it around every corner like a hound dog tracking a rabbit. Add a finger. Two, if he's horny for it. Open him right up for my throbbing cock.

My fingers glide over the tip, wet with precum, and the sensation sends a shiver up my spine. It also makes my elbow twitch, ramming into the window with a loud bang. Boone snaps around, jutting his head forward, searching for the culprit.

I quickly shimmy away from the window. The room is dark, so there's no way he can see me. My gaze darts down to the blanket on the bed. Moonlight floods the room, creating a spotlight, and dammit all the hell. Could he see me way up here? Did he?

With a deep inhale, I settle and realize my dick has grown even harder. The idea of him catching me stroking myself, thinking of him, watching him, makes my insides boil.

I count to ten, take another breath, and peek out the window. He's gone.

I lie back on the bed, resting my head on the pillow, and run my free hand down my chest, pausing to pinch my left nipple. My cock is slick with precum, and the thought of Boone bent over, quivering under my touch, brings me to the edge. The urge to come rushes up from my toes as my balls tighten. I'm so close, but I'm not ready. I release myself, moving my hands behind my head.

My dick points right at my chin, hard, dripping, and ready to launch. But years of being on my own have taught me that delaying my orgasm will only intensify it. I lock my fingers in my hair and contract the muscles to pulse my cock. A sticky bead stretches from the thin trail of hair that starts at my belly button and leads to my dick.

*... now that I know you like certain sweets.*

Boone's voice echoes in my head. There's a sweetness—a softness to him. Reminds me of the fleece blanket I used to love as a kid. Mom would insist on cleaning it every few weeks, and I'd worry it would fall apart from me loving on it too much or her scrubbing it against the washboard. It was like sleeping in the puffiest cloud.

I wonder what I'd find under that long leather apron and his clothes. Is he soft like his voice, or does all the baking and cooking create the same calluses and blisters I get from working with the animals and being outside? Damn sure would like to find out.

My eyes close, and I imagine him here. The bed isn't big enough for two. I'd swing my legs over the edge. Throw him my pillow to kneel on. Just like he was bent over the bins outside, he could pray between my legs. Worship my cock with his sweet lips while I run my thumb up and down his cheek—making sure to give that dimple plenty of attention. When he needs a breath, I'd rub my cockhead over his face, ramming it into the indentation, wishing I could fuck it.

"You like that fat cock?"

The words escape my lips as my fingers graze the back of my head, thinking of him licking the icing from my face off the tip of his finger.

"Want my load, Boone?"

He'd moan with pleasure, my dick stretching those beautiful, full lips.

That's it. I'm unable to hold back anymore. My hand pumps my shaft, the prickle of my orgasm arrives fast, and my nuts contract. I imagine fucking Boone's throat while holding onto the wavy, light brown hair on top of his head.

Hot spurts of cum splash the hair on my chest. Then my neck. One lands just below my lower lip, the salty bitterness close enough for me to taste, and I can't help but wish it was Boone's finger instead of my tongue feeding me.

After cleaning up with an old bandana I keep for this very purpose, I pull on my white tank and underwear, heading toward the bathroom with a semi hard cock to take a final piss before hitting the hay. The soft hum of the house feels heavy, like the air before a storm. As I reach for the bathroom door, it swings open, and I nearly stumble into an almost-naked Boone.

He's got a towel draped low around his waist, his hair slicked back from the shower. Water glistens on his chest, lightly dusted with hair, and my dick twitches in my boxers, quickly springing to life. He's got this perfect body, not too muscular, with just enough heft to him to make him solid. Like I could get lost digging my fingers into him. My skin tingles from wanting to touch him. His eyes meet mine, and for a second, neither of us says anything.

"Sorry," he mutters, but his voice sounds lower than usual, rougher. "I always need a shower before bed. Usually use the one closer to my room, but Benny was taking forever." He clears his throat, and his voice returns to its normal cheerful tone. "I'm a mess from cooking all day. And cleaning. And, well, it helps me relax."

I step back, but not far enough to avoid the way his damp skin seems to call to mine, the steam from the bathroom and heat radiating off him, making it hard to breathe. There's a flicker in his emerald eyes, something darker, something like hunger—like he's seeing me for the first time in a way that makes me feel exposed.

"All good," I manage.

He shifts slightly, taking a step closer, almost without

thinking. He smells like fresh pine and the faintest trace of sugar. "Need anything?" he asks, his words slow and deliberate.

Tension in the space between us, swirls thick as smoke. I shake my head, my pulse picking up. *You.* The word echoes in my head, then swims down to my throat, getting stuck.

His gaze dips down to my lips, then back up to meet my eyes. "I'm at the end of the hall," he says, voice low. "My door has the spoon on it."

My head tilts, and my lips purse, but nothing comes out.

"All the siblings have something to tell folks which room is ours. Beau's got a lasso 'cause he's in charge. Billie, a branding iron. We don't mark animals here, but it gives tattoo vibes. Benny, a saddle."

He motions to himself, his hand outlining his perfect pecs as he mimes stirring.

"A spoon. For stirring. Knock if you need anything."

The air crackles with unspoken things, and I can't tell if Boone's giving me space or daring me to close the distance. Either way, the beat of silence stretches on, like we're both waiting for something to tip the scales.

I want to step closer, but I'm afraid I'll do something I can't take back.

With a nod, I move past him and shut the bathroom door.

## 7

## BOONE

OVER THE NEXT WEEK, Wylie Anderson acclimates to life on Rainbow Ranch. After the bathroom run-in, the tension thicker than molasses in a jar, I expected him to keep his distance. But ranch life doesn't really allow it. We're all sleeping on the same floor of the house. Sharing two bathrooms. Meals. Laundry. Everything is communal here. It's the nature of ranch life.

Wylie's never late for a meal. He's polite—puts his napkin on his lap and always says please and thank you. He compliments every new dish I serve him with an adorable half smile, like a puppy having his first bite of kibble.

At breakfast one morning, knowing Wylie likes more salt than I use, I reach for it—at the exact same time as him. Our fingers brush against the cool ceramic of Ma's favorite cow shakers—white for salt, black for pepper.

"Sorry. You take it," he mumbles.

He does this thing where he dips his head whenever he speaks first.

"No, I was grabbing it for you," I reply, placing it by his plate.

We meet outside the bathroom nightly. I'm not sure if he's trained his bladder to pee at the exact moment I'm done showering or if it's just a lucky coincidence. I use the bathroom near his room, regardless of whether the one close to mine is occupied. The last person I see before retiring each night is him. And the tight tank and boxer briefs that leave very little to the imagination. My spank bank runneth over.

During breakfast on Thursday, Beau, with a smile I know all too well, says, "Wylie and I are working late."

I've heard them talking about a new paddock for Noodles. They're constructing something smaller than the existing one.

"We can finish today, but we may be late for dinner," he says.

"Noodles needs a little space to himself." Wylie adds a spot of sugar to his coffee.

He doesn't lower his head as much, and I can almost see his entire face.

"No trouble at all." I take the last waffle and dish it out to Benny, who quickly pours syrup over it and begins cutting. "Why don't I bring you lunch? It's the least I can do for... Noodles."

Billie laughs, almost choking on her waffle. "Since when do you care so much about the horses?"

I shoot her a death glare, but she only tilts her head, waiting for my reply.

"Hey, my job is to take care of all creatures on the ranch. That includes the animals."

She furrows her brow and rolls her eyes before returning to her breakfast.

After clearing the table, cleaning up, and prepping lunch, I load up my old wagon. Knowing they'll be hungry, I prepare four sandwiches and four pieces of cake, and I fill a small cooler with bottles of sweet tea and chilled water.

"Got some fresh apples and pears." Pepper plods into the kitchen, setting down a large basket of fruit.

At sixteen, Pepper, one of the teens from the foster home in Johnson Springs, already has a strong sense of self. With deep auburn-dyed hair and baggy overalls, Pepper started coming to the ranch almost two years ago. Those first few weeks, their nails were always perfectly painted—until they realized that working on a ranch doesn't exactly lend itself to manicures.

"Amazing. Can you bag up a few?" I nod to the wagon.

Pepper nods quickly, grabs a brown bag from the counter, and selects pieces to pack.

"It's for Beau and Mr. Anderson," I say. "They're building Noodles a new paddock."

"Noodles?" Pepper and the horse both arrived at the ranch within days of each other, and as a welcome gesture, Beau let them choose the horse's name.

"Yup. Mr. Anderson has been making progress with him. Slow and steady."

"The new guy? Really?"

I nod and a smile tugs at my lips.

"Why you smiling?" Pepper asks. "Oh. Oh."

"Never you mind." I empty a small bucket of ice into the cooler. "Grab me some napkins."

"Yes, sir," they say with a huge grin.

With a glance out the window over the sink, I notice the sun's high in the sky, real fierce, and even with their hats on, I reckon it's mighty hot out there. Before I head out, I quickly check my face in the bathroom mirror. Every now and then, when I catch a glimpse of myself, I swear I'm looking at Beau. When we were just knee-high to a grasshopper, we'd mess with folks, tryin' to fool them about who was who. But as the years pass, we sure do look less alike. At least to me. Strangers still tell us we're a spitting reflection of each other, though.

As I get closer to the horse barn, the new paddock in progress stretches out ahead of me, along with a mix of scattered piles. There's a heap of rough-cut wood, cans of paint stacked haphazardly, and a mound of pea stone, its smooth edges catching the light like a thousand little polished gems. Pa always swore by pea stone instead of gravel, saying it was gentler on the horses' hooves. Beau insists on using it, just like Pa did.

When I finally spot my brother and Wylie working over by the paddock, a warm sensation spreads through my body, the kind that sits heavy and sweet in your belly, like the sun on your skin after a long stretch of rain. Something about seeing them there, in the middle of all the dust and hard work, fills me with a quiet satisfaction.

"Anyone hungry?"

The wagon squeaks up to the finished portion of the fence. They've brought Noodles and tied him up under the massive oak tree, presumably for shade. Beau's holding a plank while Wylie hammers it in place. I've seen my brother do this alone, but there's something sweet about watching them collaborate and witnessing the quick progress they're making.

Wylie throws the hammer, the loud thwack echoing against the barn exterior, and I glance over at the horse, who doesn't seem fazed. When I return my gaze to him, Wylie removes his large hat, and the sweat beads off his forehead. He grabs the sleeve of his white T-shirt to wipe it.

"Here, I brought a few extra," I say, grabbing a pack of bandanas from the wagon. "For both of ya."

I pull one out and hand it to him. He's so damn sweaty that his shirt has soaked through. I should've brought extra shirts and gotten a full show.

"Thanks." He nods, then grabs the dark navy bandana, wiping it across his face and neck. Then, for the love of Dolly, he lifts his shirt and swipes at his stomach. It's covered in thick, dark hair—a rich, tangled carpet I can't help but imagine rolling through.

"You didn't have to deliver lunch." Beau takes a bandana from my hand, wiping his forehead. "I need to go to the house to get more nails anyway. Didn't expect us to get this far this fast."

"Yeah, you guys are killing it. This will definitely be done soon." I toss Beau a water from the cooler in the wagon, and he gulps half the bottle. "And it's my pleasure. It's good for me to get out in the sun occasionally."

Beau gives me a knowing smirk. "What's for lunch?"

"Sunshine," I reply with a wink. "Can't let you be the only twin with that sun-kissed glow. I'm just getting my daily dose so I don't look like the pale, leftover half."

Beau laughs, shaking his head. "Well, at least we know what's cooking. Boone sandwiches."

"You wish," I say. "Actually, your favorite. Egg salad. The hens are laying overtime and we have an abundance of eggs. Benefit to not having to buy eggs in town at those ridiculous prices. Pris says spring sun is to blame, so scream at the sky if you're not a fan."

I shrug at Wylie, attempting a smile.

"Not me. Love eggs." He eyes the bags of food in the wagon.

"Good, because you're getting French toast for dinner. Quiche for breakfast. Maybe omelets for dinner tomorrow. We'll see what I wrangle up."

Wylie looks at me with soft eyes, the faintest hint of a smile creeping up on his stubbly jaw.

Beau checks his field watch—the one he inherited from Pa—and gazes toward the sky.

"Best run and grab those nails. Check a few emails. I'll be back in twenty," he says.

I hand him a sack with two sandwiches, fruit, cake, and bottles of tea and water. My brother eats up a storm when he's working hard.

Beau shoves his shoulder on mine and gives me a quick peck on the cheek. He turns toward the main house, but before he moves, he slaps my ass—our inside joke to sass each other.

"Mr. Anderson," I say, handing him a bag.

"Care to join me?" he asks, nodding toward the tree. He gestures to Noodles, who, sensing him nearby, shakes his head, his long mane catching the breeze.

"Sure, I've got a few minutes."

There's never really down time on the ranch, but even I need to eat. Dragonflies swarm in my stomach as I grasp the handle of the wagon and roll it under the oak. Noodles takes a tentative step back as the wheels squeak, and I make sure to park it as far as possible from him while keeping it in the shade.

"Damn wheels sound like they're about to fall off," I say. "Sorry about that. Not trying to scare him."

"Just needs a little oil. I can lube it up for ya tonight."

My eyes go wide, but Mr. Anderson doesn't appear to notice or get the humor in what he's offered.

"You don't have to do that. I'll get Winnie to do it."

He shrugs, then mumbles, "Suit yourself. More than happy to, though."

Happy. I'm not sure I've heard him use that word since

he arrived just over a week ago. There's been the occasional trace of a smile. A laugh. But nothing to show he's actually content here on the ranch.

"Okay. Winnie's gonna be busy peeling potatoes. Hash browns, for the eggs." I grab the cooler and place it near the tree, sitting next to it.

He nods, and the smile that's been doing its best to stay undercover breaks free. I swear I spot a few teeth, and my own mouth, unable to contain itself, kicks up. We're under the tree, two grown men exchanging goofy grins like kids on Christmas morning.

"Sit." I pat the short grass next to me. The shade keeps it from growing as tall as the rest of the field. "If you want."

Wylie removes his hat, places it on the handle of the wagon, and joins me. He's sprawled out, legs wide and leaning back, like he's hoping a swift breeze will arrive any moment.

"Always cooler under the tree." I take a plate from the wagon and start unpacking items for his lunch. "As kids, we used to spend a lot of time here under the guise of staying cool. We were also trying to avoid chores. We had climbing contests." I lean back like Wylie, my eyes tracking the trunk up to the long branches covered in new leaves. "Billie always won. She climbed higher than all three of us boys. Higher and faster." A lopsided grin takes over my face. "She'd stay up there daydreaming for hours. Beau and I would end up laying here." My hand grazes the grass where we're sitting.

"There." Wylie reaches over the plate I've set before him, his index finger drifting toward my face. He doesn't touch me, but there's a spark between his skin and mine, something electric that leaves me breathless for a split second.

"Do I have something on my face?"

I already checked, of course—just to be sure. But maybe I missed something.

"Flour? I made bread this morning, and the flour was flying everywhere. Me and that rolling pin have been known to tussle."

He shakes his head, a small smile yanking at the corner of his lips.

"Nah. This. Right here."

His eyes meet mine, searching, asking, and I give a barely perceptible nod. Then, with a tenderness I wasn't prepared for, his finger touches the curve of my cheek, tracing the soft dip of the indentation I forget is even there.

"You have this dimple," he murmurs, his touch lingering for a moment longer than necessary, as if it's a secret he's just discovered. My breath catches in my chest at the closeness. And for a heartbeat, everything else falls away—the partially built paddock, Noodles breathing ten feet away, the entire world—and it's just us, quiet under the tree.

## 8

## WYLIE

MY DAMN FINGER is on Boone Adams' face.

If all the late-night bathroom hallway stalking didn't clue the cookie in that I'm sweet on him, this oughtta drive the point home.

I lift my gaze to check his expression as a slight tremor in my hand betrays my hesitation, but Boone leans ever so slightly into my touch. He's so damn sweet.

Noodles grunts, and I pull my hand into my lap.

"Sorry, didn't mean to..."

"Mr. Ander... Wylie." He reaches for my hand, but I pick up a sandwich, avoiding his touch.

Boone licks his lips as his chest expands with a deep breath.

"Is he okay?" He nods towards Noodles.

"Yeah. Grunting means he's relaxed is all. Wouldn't be surprised if he closed his eyes and took a nap."

"Good day for a nap." Boone removes his hat and leans back against the tree. The brim isn't as large as mine, but no way can he rest his head with it on.

"Not eating?" I ask.

I take a bite of the sandwich and a moan escapes my lips.

"Not hungry yet. But glad you're enjoying it."

"The bread. It's tangy. Earthy. But there's a subtle sweetness."

"That's sourdough. I'm glad someone appreciates all the time and effort that goes into it."

"And this egg salad... fuck me."

This elicits a laugh from Boone.

"Sorry," I mumble, holding my hand over my mouth.

"Don't apologize for enjoying my food." He hands me a napkin. "Ever."

A sliver of sunlight pierces the shade of the tree, highlighting the sparkle in his green eyes, and I'm so tempted to touch him again.

"What's in this?" I ask, covering my full mouth trying not to appear like an uncouth swine.

"Eggs. Mayo. Diced onion... Dijon. A few secret ingredients..."

He leans forward and glances around.

"Promise not to tell?"

Who the fuck am I telling about his egg salad? Jesse James?

I nod.

"A little lemon juice. Dill and chives. Some people add dill, but it's the dill *and* the chives that creates that explosion in your mouth."

A chuckle escapes my very full mouth, and I grab the napkin in my lap and blanket my lips. Is this guy for real? Explosion in his mouth? Is he trying to yank my chain?

"What's so funny?"

"Nothing. You're just..." I don't say how damn cute he is, how I want to smash my face into his—I shake my head.

Boone grabs a water from the cooler, twists the cap off and takes a long swig.

"So, Mr. Anderson," he says, that dimple making a cameo as I try to focus on finishing my sandwich. "You're welcome to stay as long as you like here with our family. But where's yours?"

"Back in Wyoming. What's left of 'em, anyway."

"What happened?" Boone's voice comes out softer. Lower.

The snowstorm. Pop. Luke. It all roars in my head like the wild winds on the open plains, and I close my eyes, trying to push it away.

"Nothing... haven't talked to them in a spell."

"Oh. I'm sorry."

Our eyes meet, and Boone gives this half smile, like he understands without me having to spill it.

"He favors you." He glances over to Noodles, who's nibbling on the grass. "Hasn't been out of his stall much since he threw Beau."

"He just needed the right person."

"You."

"Maybe. We'll see, I s'pose."

"Do you think he'll let you ride him?"

We're both watching Noodles. He's lowered his head, and the muscles in his legs are twitching. He's ready to sleep.

Even though Boone's eyes are on the horse, I shrug.

"Don't know. Hope so. Sometimes horses need time."

"We all do," Boone says.

"What about you? You like to ride?"

Boone's eyebrows shoot up, like I asked him to rope a bull with one hand and chug a bottle of whiskey with the other. I can't figure out what's running through his head.

"Horses," I say. "All your siblings seem fond of 'em."

"Well, sadly, the equine gene skipped me. Pa used to joke that Beau got all the horse skills in the womb."

My lips crack into a grin thinking of the two of them knocking knees inside their Ma's belly.

"I tried riding when we were kids. The horses never took to me like they did with Beau. And I was always hanging around Ma's ankles, trying to help in the kitchen. Beau and Pa. Boone and Ma. That's how it always was. When Billie and Benny came along, they both were inclined to be out with Pa and Beau."

"What happened to 'em? Your folks?" I ask, and the moment the words escape my mouth, a wince overtakes my face. This is why I don't talk too much. Always saying ignorant things.

"Sorry. Don't mean to pry."

"No, I asked about your family." Boone takes my empty plate and places it in a tub inside his wagon.

"It was a car accident. Seven years ago. They were on their way back from a weekend in Tulsa—celebrating their anniversary. We all chipped in for the hotel and a fancy dinner out. I can still hear Ma complaining about it for weeks before. Nothing to wear, she said. And why spend all that money on a place to stay and food when we've got everything we need right here? It was classic Ma, always looking for an excuse to make things harder than they had to be."

Boone lets out a bitter puff of air, like a quiet snort, almost like what Noodles does when he's frustrated. "Anyway, after the wreck... it's just been us. We've run the ranch on our own ever since. But we've got each other. And honestly, it's not only the Adams siblings anymore. We've built something more. We've built a family here. Even if it's not how I thought things would turn out, it's a good thing. A damn good thing, all things considered."

Well, I'll be damned. This guy's something else. Been through all that and still wears a grin like the sun's always shinin' on him. Doesn't seem like anything would rattle him. Like he's made of somethin' tougher than leather. Hell, I wish I had a speck of the gumption and spirit he's got. But I don't. Truth be told, I'm a whole lotta things, but brave isn't one of 'em.

I ran. Took off when the shit hit the fan and hid my tail instead of standin' tall. Guess I'm not half the man Boone Adams is—or deserves. But damn, I sure wish I were.

My head shakes the slightest bit.

"Don't mean to rain on the rodeo," he says. "Better have dessert before Beau returns."

He reaches into the wagon, pulling an aluminum foil-covered plate out.

"Cake." Boone raises his eyebrows. "A prairie dog pup told me you like it."

"That so?"

"Yup. I brought you a few pieces. Eat what you like. We can wrap and save the rest."

He peels the foil back, and the plate overflows with cake. Five or six pieces. It's hard to make out with the icing piled high.

"Vanilla cake. White icing." He holds the plate up, and the sugary smell makes my mouth water. "Hope that's okay."

"Fuck, Boone. This all for me?"

He nods, the familiar dimple making another appearance as he carefully plates a piece and hands me a fork with a smile. His eyes linger on me, watching intently as I take the first bite. I make a point of savoring it, exaggerating my pleasure just enough for him to notice, my expression giving away how good it is. As I pull the fork away, I deliberately leave a small dab of icing on my lower lip, a playful little tease, hoping it'll catch his eye.

I pause before taking another bite. Boone cocks his head, giving me a shit-eating grin as he stares.

"What? Something on my face?" I ask.

He leans in, his fingers brushing lightly over my lower lip as he swipes the icing, bringing it toward his mouth. But before he can taste it, I catch his wrist, guiding his finger to my lips. Without a pause, I take it into my mouth, gently sucking the sweet icing off, my gaze never leaving his.

The silence is broken only by the faint chirping of birds in the distance. Boone leans in closer, his finger still in my mouth, the space between us narrowing.

Noodles suddenly blows air through his nostrils, stomping his feet, making the ground shake.

Boone pulls his finger away, grinning. "I thought he was ready for a nap," he says with a laugh.

"Me too." I stand and walk toward Noodles.

His ears are slightly forward, twitching with curiosity. The muscles on his back seem tense, and he shifts his weight from one hoof to another. Carefully, I step closer, and his nostrils flare, inhaling deeply. There's a scent in the air—something he knows or wants, but what?

"Good boy," I whisper. "You hungry?"

I bend over and pick up the cake, removing the fork and placing it on the ground.

Noodles' large, soft eyes narrow, his gaze flicking from my face to the cake in my hands.

He takes a tentative step back, unsure, but as he sniffs the air again, his tail swishes. The way he's studying the cake in my hand, I'd say he's concentrating. The temptation is there, but uncertainty lingers—like he wants me closer but isn't sure the risk is worth it.

I pause at his hesitation, waiting for a sign.

"Cake?" Boone whispers from the grass at the base of the tree. "He can't want my cake."

I hold the plate up slowly, not wanting to scare Noodles. He watches, his muscles taut with caution. But the smell of Boone's sweet confection is undeniable now, and the horse's resolve weakens.

"Is it safe?" Boone asks.

I give a nod.

"Vanilla's good. Usually, too much sugar isn't the best choice, and chocolate's off limits, but if Noodles is hankerin' for a taste, I'm not about to stand in his way."

He edges a little closer, his nostrils twitching, smelling as his ears flick back and forth.

Then, just as he's about to reach the cake, Noodles stops, sniffs again, and takes a small step back.

"It's okay, boy."

I lift the plate, and slowly, his lips curl up. His tongue flicks out, teasing the icing.

As he keeps licking, I inch the plate closer, and after a few more swipes, he takes a dainty bite, leaving half the slice untouched. He chews, swallows, and lets out a satisfied nicker.

"He likes it." Boone's voice cuts through the quiet, sudden like a rogue tumbleweed in a calm breeze. I didn't see him get up or cross over, but here he is, standing right behind me.

Noodles turns his head, content with his taste, giving me a look like he knows he's just had the best treat of his life.

"He does," I say, turning toward Boone. "Hard not to. Sweetest cake baked by the sweetest cookie."

Boone flashes a smile, stepping closer, but the sound of Beau's boots crunching on the gravel signals the end of my lunch break.

"Well, I'd best get back to the kitchen," he says, tipping his chin toward the house. "Dinner won't cook itself."

I grab my hat from the wagon's handle, settle it on my head, and give him a small nod, tipping the brim.

I want to thank him for everything—lunch, the company, the cake—but all I can muster is, "Much obliged."

"My pleasure."

Boone Adams gives me a wink. With a squeal of the wagon's wheels, he begins hauling it back toward the house, his boots stirring up a cloud of dust. I watch him go, my chest tight, like something's caught in there—stuck between a knot and a flutter. It's an unsettling feeling, the kind that doesn't sit right... but I hope it never leaves.

## 9

## BOONE

WYLIE ANDERSON'S COURTING ME. Or his version of it. He's got this slow, clumsy sort of charm, but there's something about him that makes me wonder if there's more on his mind than he lets on.

After dinner, he doesn't leave the table when I shoo Winnie away to let me finish prepping the pastry for tomorrow's quiche. Sometimes a man needs to be alone with his dough. Everyone else finishes their evenings with late night animal visits, card games in the den, or telling stories around the fire out back. I enjoy having the last few hours of my day alone in the kitchen.

Lifting the food processor from the shelf on the open island, I breathe in the cool air drifting in from the back door. Ma's simple pie crust recipe doesn't take long to prepare, but the secret is letting it rest overnight in the fridge. With the rest of the ingredients gathered on the counter, I begin dicing the chilled butter into small cubes.

When I lift the knife to slice, I'm interrupted by the sound of a throat clearing.

Wylie stands at the doorway between the dining room

and kitchen, leaning against the molding with a sheepish look on his face.

"Mr. Anderson, come in if you like. No snakes in here. None that will bite you, anyway."

I raise my eyebrows at him, and his lips stretch into a wide handsome smile.

"Sit," I nod to the stool in the corner, and for all that's good and mighty, I sound like Ma ordering him around.

Once my mortification subsides, a smirk sneaks onto my face. Mr. Anderson does as I say, doing his best not to squirm as he watches me prepare the ice water.

"Another mighty fine meal," he says. "Best dang French toast I've ever had."

"Thank you, sir." I wink and scoop ice cubes from the freezer into the stainless steel bowl I've retrieved. "A little cinnamon and vanilla in the batter." I shrug, unsure he cares about my French toast recipe.

"You really..." he starts but then stops, and when I look at him, his jaw appears fixed and almost closed. The stubble on his face has gotten longer, and I wonder what his face might look like clean-shaven.

Placing the ice on the counter, I take a step closer to him. I'm inclined to ask what he meant to say, but I don't. Instead, I search Wylie's face, his deep brown eyes, and see he's pondering where to go from here. So, I wait.

He bites his lower lip, perhaps in frustration, and I take another step.

"Take your time," I whisper. "I'm not going anywhere."

He takes a deep breath, and when his eyes find mine, I curl the left side of my mouth up.

"Care," he says, his voice scarcely more than a breath.

Wylie's jaw remains firm, and I open my mouth to reply, but before I can, he continues.

"You really care. With all..." He nods toward the counter. "This."

Fireflies light up in my chest because, even though I know everyone on the ranch appreciates each other, we're not big on saying it.

He's staring at me like he can see right to my core, and his voice comes out low and deep. "Damn, you're..."

Out of nowhere, my head feels woozy. Like those damn fireflies in my chest took a sharp turn north and are now fluttering in my head. I move to the counter to brace myself as the room spins like my trusty mixer.

"Boone."

He's behind me. Hands around my waist, firm chest against my back. Holding me.

"If I weren't already dizzy, I'd be swooning," I say.

This makes him laugh, and as the room settles back into place, he guides me over to the stool.

"Sit." He nods at the stool.

He carefully removes my hat and places it on the counter.

"Now, who's bossing who around?"

He turns and grabs a glass from the open shelving above the sink, quickly scooping ice from the bowl on the counter and filling the glass at the sink.

"Drink."

"I'm fine." I feel the color return to my face as I grip the glass with both hands and sip.

He's crouching before me, his brown hair dusting his forehead. My fingers twitch on the cool tumbler, yearning to brush it out of his face.

I take a drink, making sure my tongue isn't too dry, before speaking.

"I'm not used to cowboys..."

"Your twin brother's a cowboy. Younger brother, too. Your sister's got more grit than most men. Hell, you're downright surrounded by cowboys."

"I was going to say, I'm not used to cowboys being sweet on me."

Wylie draws his lips in. He's on his knees now, the heels of his boots off the ground. He takes a long draw of air through his nose and then places a hand on my knee.

My eyes stare at his fingers, rough from riding. I recognize the dry brittleness of my siblings' skin, and I know a few tricks to keep the calluses at bay, but I keep my mouth shut and take another swallow.

"Boone, can I ask you something?"

He tilts his head, a grin tugging at the corner of his mouth.

"Well, seems like you got me cornered."

A slow smile creeps across my face as the warmth of his hand on my knee keeps me in place. Then, with a bit of pressure, those fingers squeeze the muscle at the base of my thigh—enough to send a shiver all the way up my spine.

"Why are you by yourself?"

I take a gulp of water, and the ice creates a jam near my teeth.

"I'm not. I've got my brothers and Billie. Pris, Winnie. The teens come to help and… I take care of them."

"That's not what I mean."

My butt scooches back on the stool, and the wall meets my back. There's nowhere to go and nothing left for me to say.

"You take care of them. But who takes care of you?"

Wylie's hand abandons my knee and brushes against my cheek. His finger pushes a loose strand of hair out of the way and then traces down my jawline, pausing under my lower lip.

"I've been wantin' to kiss you for a good while now."

My mind storms—thoughts crashing into one another like the beaters in my mixer, too tangled to make any sense. Everything blurs but his face. Without a second thought, driven by a longing and something deeper I can't put my finger on, I close the space between us. Our mouths are so near, and the warmth of his breath ghosts over my lips.

"This... okay?" My voice feels unsteady, unsure, even as confidence builds inside me.

Wylie doesn't answer right away, just looks at me, his gaze steady, like he's searching for something. His breath caresses my face, and the way he shifts closer without speaking tells me everything I need to know.

"Yeah," he says quietly, his voice rough as his pupils blow wide.

That's all it takes. I lean forward, and my lips brush against his. The kiss is soft, tentative at first, as if we're both testing the waters. Having my lips on Wylie Anderson's does something to my insides—makes 'em soft and mushy like fresh batter. But then the tension breaks and something shifts, like we've been waiting for this moment since the day he arrived.

He leans into me, his hands resting on my shoulders. The touch is affectionate and firm, grounding me. I deepen the kiss, my heart hammering in my chest like a woodpecker on caffeine, and everything else disappears. There's no room for doubts, no space for hesitation. The entire ranch fades away, leaving only the press of his lips against mine as the pulse of our hearts sync.

Wylie's hand never leaves my face, but he folds his fingers around the back of my neck, holding me in place.

His rough stubble presses against the skin around my mouth as his tongue pokes at my lips. Without hesitation, I welcome him in, softly sucking on his tongue, urging him deeper.

"Fuck," he murmurs into my mouth.

I pull back, taking a moment to really see him, his eyes, the set of his stubbly jaw, the way his lips tinge pink from the attention. He's so darn handsome, it hurts.

"Hopefully later," I say.

He laughs. The biggest, heartiest chuckle I've heard from him in the time he's been here, and a jolt of excitement zips through me.

Before he's able to speak, I place my empty glass on the counter and reach behind his head, pulling him back, this time thrusting my tongue between his teeth. Wylie lets out a soft moan, revealing a tenderness that makes my dick jump to life in my jeans. There's a light touch, almost a whisper against my skin, starting at my cheek, continuing around my ear, and ending with a gentle kneading of my earlobe.

Of course I know we can't stay like this forever—him kneeling before me, kissing me on the kitchen stool, out in the open for anyone to see. Still, I wish I could freeze this moment. Make it last forever.

When we finally pull back, just a few inches, our foreheads resting together, we're both breathless.

"You know, I came back here for a reason," he says, his voice hushed but steady.

"To kiss me?"

"To fix your wagon."

"Oh."

"Kissing is a bonus." His finger lands on my dimple, making tiny circles.

"Wagon's out back." I nod toward the rear door. "I need to finish my pastry before bed."

He nods, pulling his lips in as he scans my face, searching.

"I'll grab oil from the shed."

I nod, and Wylie moves his hand to the ground, bracing himself to stand.

"Wait," I say. "One more."

"You sure?"

I look at him, my chest tight with emotion.

"Never been more," I reply, my breath catching in my throat. I press my lips to his, tasting like sweet tea, a kiss that consumes my very being.

# 10

## WYLIE

I'M up with the rooster. Slept like a horse—passing out for a little, and then wide awake all night. Rest overtaken by thoughts of Boone Adams, wearing that leather apron, hat hitched back, barely able to keep the few rogue waves of hair contained, woozy. In my arms. On the stool. His luscious lips on mine. The sweet scent of sugar and butter engulfing us in our own little bubble in the corner of the kitchen.

The rock hard boner in my skivvies presents me with a choice. Stay in bed and jerk off before breakfast, or get up and take care of what I promised him last night. Meant to do it after the kissing but was way too distracted.

I quickly get dressed and pull on my boots, knowing I've got plenty of time, and head straight for the barn. Benny is usually out just before breakfast, but I've made a habit of being the first one Noodles sees each morning. Gotta show up consistently if I wanna earn his trust.

Noodles snorts as I approach his stall.

"Good boy," I murmur.

I move slowly, letting him make the first move. Before I even raise my hand, he steps forward, nudging my shoulder.

"Oh, you want some attention this morning, huh?"

I reach out to rub his nose, and he flares his nostrils and curls his upper lip. Without overthinking it, I lean down and plant a quick kiss on his nose.

It's soft, warm—makes my insides cozy at the connection. He nickers gently, and for a brief moment, there's something unspoken between us.

When Noodles whinnies, a few other horses join in, and I take it as his way of saying he approves.

Something nudges my thigh—Dennis. The latch on his stall is broken, and he's able to let himself out. Beau mentioned fixing it, but I think everyone likes him being able to make mischief at will.

"Good morning, Dennis. No, the world hasn't forgotten about you." I hold his muzzle in my hands and give him a good scratch.

"Alright, let's clean up this stall, and then I'll brush you both. Sound good?"

Noodles bumps my head with his muzzle, nearly knocking my hat off, and I chuckle as I grab the muck fork and get to work.

As I replace the bedding with fresh shavings, the air thick with the scent of pine and earth, I hear boots approaching. The sound joins the scrape of my rake against the dirt floor.

"You're making me look bad."

It's Benny. His dark curls escape the front of his hat as he walks over.

"Just need a little peace and quiet with him," I say, leaning the rake against the wall and giving Noodles' flank a gentle pat.

"He's coming along nicely." Benny hands me an apple, which Noodles wraps his lips around, slobbering as he gobbles it.

I nod and run my hand through his soft mane. "He's been a good boy for me."

"You two are quite the pair. We're lucky to have you."

I smile. "Reckon I'm the lucky one," I reply, gently stroking his withers.

"Reckon so." He winks and walks over to Sassafras, a beautiful chestnut mare.

Once Noodles and Dennis have a good brushing, I head over to the shed, grab the WD-40, and make my way toward the main house. It's still too early for breakfast, but I know a certain cookie will be in the kitchen, preparing a feast. My gut does a little flip just thinkin' about seeing his smiling face—and that dimple.

When I'm in the dining room, music from the kitchen blasts, and I hear a faint murmuring. I move as close as I can, staying out of sight through the doorway.

"Your shakin' ass has an extra hitch in it this morning."

A voice, which I think belongs to Winnie, teases.

"Good song is all."

Boone.

Hearing him makes my stomach do a slow roll, like a calf caught in a tangled rope. He's got this cheery tone to his voice that's like sunshine after a long storm—bright, warm, and somehow, it makes everything seem a little lighter. It's that easy way he has of making you feel like the most important person in the world, like you've just been handed a cold drink on a hot day. Something about that voice, steady and strong, makes my pulse quicken, my body warm.

"Maybe it'll get you to grate that cheese a little quicker.

Gotta get these into the oven in five if we wanna have something to serve at breakfast."

I do my best to conceal the shit-eating grin painted on my face, and I hold the oil can behind my back and knock on the side of the doorway.

"Mr. Anderson." Boone gives me a single nod.

He's standing over four pie shells, filling them from a large bowl.

"Breakfast isn't for almost an hour. Quiches gotta bake."

I'm not entirely sure what quiche is, but if Boone's the one makin' it, you can bet I'll be eatin' it.

"If you're hungry," Winnie says, abandoning her grater and plate of cheese, "we've got some peach scones. I think we're saving 'em for lunch, but you're more than welcome to have one to tide you over."

"No, all good." I pat my stomach. "Just wanted to take care of your wagon."

I hold the can up and shake it.

"Right out back." Boone flicks his head toward the exit.

The wooden screen door's there, likely to keep the flies out, and I take a step toward it. But for some damn reason, my body decides to take a detour. Instead of heading straight for the door, I move toward Boone, who's back at the counter, filling his pie shells with what I reckon is some egg and veggie mix. I rest my hand on the counter for a second, before leaning in and planting a soft kiss on his cheek—quick, like it's the most natural thing in the world.

I don't linger, though. I pull back and head for the door with a quick step. It shuts behind me with a solid bang, the sound echoing in the quiet morning as I make my way out.

My heart's thumping like a drum as the sun starts to rise, painting the sky in all sorts of colors. I'm not sure what I was thinking—hell, maybe I wasn't thinking at all. But after last night, holding him, kissing him, and spending most of the night turning and twisting, thinking about him—I can't act like nothing happened. Kissing Boone Adams shifts the ground beneath my boots.

Sure enough, just outside, the wagon's sitting by the house. While it won't take more than ten minutes to oil up the axles, I'm in no hurry. I'll find a way to stretch it out, maybe fiddle with the damn thing a little longer than I need to, just so I can be out here a bit longer—and closer to him.

I grab an old milk crate from a pile nearby and pull the screwdrivers from my back pocket. Planting myself near the wagon, I flip it over. When I turn the wheels, the familiar squeaking fills the air.

"Mr. Anderson."

Boone's behind the screen door. Without looking, I can feel his eyes on my back.

The sound of the door closing, clearly in a more controlled manner as the wood gently slaps this time, and he's here. Behind me.

"You've got some nerve."

My face tightens, muscles pulling like I've just sunk my teeth into one of those hot wings, the kind that'll burn all the way down to your toes. My eyes narrow, and my jaw sets like stone, the corners of my mouth turning down as I fight to escape the sting of embarrassment crawling up from deep inside. I can feel it, sharp and tight, but I don't let it show. Hell, I'm damn glad I'm facing away from him right now, 'cause I don't want him seeing this.

"Pardon?" I poke at the spokes, not for any reason other than to give my fingers something to do.

"Prancing into my kitchen and kissing me like that."

"Prancing?" I turn to face him.

He's got his arms crossed in front of his chest, his apron

bunching up, and when my eyes land on his face, I spot that dimple—my first clue he's yankin' my chain.

"Yes, prancing."

"Sorry, won't do it again," I say, standing.

"Please don't." He takes a step toward me, arms still folded.

My hands are occupied with the oil can and screwdrivers, but when Boone Adams slowly advances, light stubble on his jawline catching the rising sun, I drop everything and grab him by the straps of his apron.

"I won't kiss you like that again," I whisper.

"Good."

His eyes find mine, making my insides smolder like campfire embers. Why can't I be around this man without wanting to have my mouth on his?

"How 'bout like this?" I ask.

The quiet of the morning surrounds us, only the faint sounds of the ranch waking up in the distance accompany the sound of our breathing. Without speaking, I step closer, my hand cupping Boone's face gently as my thumb skates up to his cheekbone. He exhales a soft breath, his lips parting ever so slightly, like he knows what's coming.

I lean in carefully, not rushing. In the light of day, I want to savor the moment. My lips hover over his, and electricity from his skin sends a tiny shock to my mouth. And then, like a whispered promise, Boone's lips meet mine.

Memories of last night flood back, intensifying my yearning to draw him closer. I yank on his apron, my breath heavy, smashing our bodies together.

Pulling back, his lips still hovering above mine, Boone whispers, "Like it rough, cowboy?"

Now why he'd have to go and say that? My cock surges

to life in my jeans, and with how I'm gripping him close, he's got to feel it.

I let out a loud puff of air through my nostrils and give a slow nod. Hell, with him, it feels like a stallion buckin' loose—something deep inside me just breaks free, ready to run wild.

"You said an hour 'til breakfast," I say, not sure what I'm implying, because this isn't how I typically roll.

I want him so bad it hurts.

"Yeah, but I've got more work to do."

He leans in, brushes a kiss across my nose, then comes back to my lips. He's gentle, and though our bodies are tangled, he pulls back.

"I'll get the wagon in tip-top shape," I say, giving him a wink as I ease my hands off of his apron straps and step back.

Before I can return to the crate, Boone grabs the front of my shirt, yanking me forward with a sudden, forceful yank. My hat slips back, almost tumbling off my head.

He leans in, his lips finding mine in a deep kiss, catching me off guard for a second.

When he pulls away, his grin's all sharp edges and slow heat. "Now, I've got biscuits to bake."

I catch my breath, nodding, and stumble back toward the wagon, but Boone stays rooted, lingering.

I stop myself and turn back to him, remembering what I've got planned for Noodles today, and maybe hoping to keep him out here another minute. "Any chance I could get a few pieces of that cake after breakfast?"

He cocks an eyebrow, giving me that sideways smile. "I thought you didn't fancy sweets. Now you want a whole plate of my cake?"

I scratch the back of my neck, feeling a little awkward

but sticking to it. "Well, it's for Noodles. We've been walking the paddock for days now, and he's starting to trust me. I'm thinking of trying to mount him this morning... and I've got a hunch that some cake might make him a bit more agreeable."

Boone's face twists in disbelief, and he stares at me like I'm crazy. "You want more of my cake for the *horse?*"

I shrug, the stubble on my chin tickling my finger as I scratch it. "Well, yeah. Might sweeten the deal."

He laughs, shaking his head, then eyes me with that same dangerous amusement. "How 'bout we make a deal?"

My curiosity piques, and I narrow my eyes. "What kind of deal?"

He steps a little closer, voice low, like he's telling me a secret. "Meet me after dinner tomorrow night. There's something I wanna show you."

I cross my arms, smirking. "Boone, I'd gladly meet you, cake or not."

His grin widens, the corners of his eyes crinkling as his gaze sharpens, like a hawk zeroing in on its prey.

"So we got ourselves a deal?"

I feel the heat stir in my chest, and my lips turn up in the faintest smile. "Deal."

## 11

## BOONE

"YOU'VE GOT an extra giddy-up in your step this morning."

Billie's on the stool, watching me stir the milk, butter, and vanilla into a massive bowl of beaten eggs.

"Do I?" I ask. "I mean, who doesn't love waffles? They're like crispy pancakes with ridges. There's so much more real estate for syrup. What's not to love?"

I glance at my little sister. She's not so little anymore, but in my mind, she'll always be the one chasing after Beau and me, nipping at our heels. Her open flannel is rolled up past her elbows, exposing a good portion of the tattoos covering her arms. Billie's always been the one to call us boys on our shit, and the look on her face warns me this morning will be no different.

"Yeah, waffles are life." She pulls her feet up on the stool, trying to fit like she did when she was little, and she mostly manages it. "But, I'm thinking it might have more to do with a certain cowboy payin' you a little extra attention."

I pour the egg mixture into the dry ingredients, grab my oversized whisk, and get to work. The waffle iron sizzles in anticipation. Knowing the crew will be showing up shortly, with four dozen waffles to prepare, helps keep my focus.

"So, I'm right about you and Mr. Anderson? Winnie called it the day he arrived."

I steal a glance as Billie's massive, mischievous grin sprawls across her face.

"He's..." I pause, pouring the first batch into the hot grooves, the crackling and sweet aroma instantly filling the room.

"Hot," she says. "Quiet. Maybe a little mysterious."

She points her finger at me and marks imaginary boxes. "Check, check, check..."

I shrug and close the top of the waffle iron. Unable to argue with her, I set the timer for three minutes.

"I'm happy for you, Boonie." She's up, hugging me from behind. "You take such good care of us, and it's time you had someone to return the favor."

"We take care of each other," I say, turning around so she's in my arms. "And anyway, I'm not the only single sibling around here. Heard from Rosa lately?"

Billie and Rosa had been inseparable forever, both top cowgirls in their own right—until Rosa left a year ago to join the traveling rodeo.

"We're talking about you right now." She places a hand on my chest, and I stare down at the cactus inked on her forearm.

Even after Billie was old enough to choose to work with Pa and Beau, she'd sneak into the kitchen, taking my spot on the stool to talk my ear off about horses. She's a grown-ass woman now. Fiercer than I'll ever be, but I still love having her tucked into my torso this way. I'll always be her big brother, no matter what.

"Boonie, I know you don't want to hear it, but you need a little attention... down here."

She tries to slap my ass, but I grab her, doing my best to hold her still, but she's like a wild mare trying to stretch her legs. I may be a good foot taller, but Billie's always been stronger.

"My butt is just fine," I tease, slapping her on the bottom.

"It will be after Mr. Anderson gets ahold of it."

We're laughing loudly now—the room resembles a lively cattle round-up, but I've moved us away from the scorching waffle iron. Billie grips both my wrists with one hand, and I struggle to break free as she grabs for my hat. Ma used to call it roughhousing, and nobody does it better than Billie.

"Ahold of what?"

The sound of Wylie's low voice cuts through our guffawing, and we freeze. Before either of us can respond, the metallic clanging noise of the timer fills the kitchen.

"Waffles!" I yell and untangle myself from my sister to pry the first batch out.

"Everyone loves waffles." Billie tips her hat to Wylie and scurries out to the dining room.

"Mornin'," Wylie says with a dip of his chin.

He moves closer, but since I'm catching my breath as I fork hot waffles out of the iron, he stays a good foot away from me.

"Hungry?" I ask. "I've got a few more batches to make, but maybe you could take these to the table for me while they're hot?"

I hold the platter up, only partially covered with golden-brown waffles, their steam rising slightly. I'll use a smaller plate to ferry fresh ones as I make them.

"Course." He takes the dish from me, and his fingers brush against mine.

His eyes, pools of dark brown, hold mine, and I try my darndest to maintain my composure as my face warms.

Between Wylie and the piping hot waffle iron, I'm about to melt.

He steps toward the dining room, and wanting to keep him near for another minute, I blurt, "Got another cake plate all wrapped and ready to go. I left it on the buffet. Your name's on it."

With a playful wink, I send him off. Instead of leaving, he rushes forward, the aroma of the waffles palpable as he cradles them carefully to the side with one hand. And sure enough, Wylie Anderson plants the sweetest kiss right on my cheek. He presses just enough for his stubble to brush against my skin, and I swear, if I weren't leaning against the counter, my legs would give out.

"See you tonight." His voice, a low rumble, vibrates against my ear.

My heart skips a beat—like the universe is holding its breath—then that darn waffle iron sizzles, reminding me there are more mouths to feed and bringing me back to reality.

12

———

WYLIE

WITH THE NEW paddock built for Noodles, I spend a good portion of my days with him, just sitting there in the quiet, letting him get used to the space. It's a good-sized lot, plenty of room for him to roam and graze, but he's still a little skittish, like a squirrel on a wire. Beau's not sure what he's been through, but whatever it is, it's left him leery of folks, so I don't push him too hard. I know it'll take time.

I talk to him, soft and low, like I've done with every animal who's ever needed a little extra patience. "It's okay," I say, steady as I can, holdin' out the lead rope far enough so he knows I'm close but not a threat. His giant brown eyes flicker over to me, but he doesn't come any closer. He backs up a step, his tail swishing like he's not sure what to make of this whole *human* thing.

I let him have his space, sitting down on the fence rail. The sun peeks out behind fluffy clouds, casting him in a beautiful light, but Noodles doesn't seem to care. I'd love to take a picture of him and show him what a handsome boy he is. He's all too aware of the world around him, his ears

89

twitching at every little sound. After a while, I get up slow and easy, careful not to make any quick moves, and I take a few steps toward him. He flinches but doesn't bolt—just a little side-step, like he's weighing his options.

I hold out the lead rope again, barely close enough that he could sniff it if he wanted. "Come on, boy," I murmur, "ain't nothing to be afraid of."

I lift my hand, palm facing him. His nostrils flare, and for a minute, I think he might run off. But then he takes a step closer—and pushes his muzzle forward into my hand.

I keep my voice calm, my movements steady. He sniffs my skin, lips twitching and tickling my hand as a soft breeze stirs the tall grass, and for a moment, a hush falls over the ranch.

"Good boy," I say. "Got a sweet treat for you."

I hop over the fence and walk to the tree where I've left my belongings. The morning sun has me down to my tank top. I left my flannel shielding the cake, and when I uncover it, the foil glistens in the beam of sunlight poking through the leaves.

There right on the foil, Boone's written my name with a fat black marker. He's made a smiley face for the dot on top of the 'i', and I huff a laugh thinking about him putting it there—for me.

I don't pay much attention to love. Never been around long enough for it to take root, I reckon. Life's been a saddlebag full of dust and distance, too busy with the next job to worry about feelings. Sure, there've been a few men along the way. A night here, a quickie there. Folks would probably call 'em flings, but I don't much care for labels. It's just the way it goes.

One night, we're two bodies sharing the same fire, swapping stories and laughing like it means something. And then, when the stars burn out and the sun rises, it's over. No promises, no strings.

When the time comes, I pack up my gear, head for the highway, and hitch to the next stop. Ain't no use holding onto something that ain't meant to stay. Love's for folks with time to spare, and I've never been one to slow down for it. The next job's always calling, and I'm always answering.

But there's something about this place that's got me second-guessing. The ranch. The people. The cookie— Boone Adams. I've never been one to let myself get tangled up in anyone or anything. So why in the hell does this feel different? It's like the land itself has a pull on me, something I can't shake. Something I don't wanna quit. Every time I think about leaving, the damn feeling gnaws at my gut, like I'd miss something. Like maybe—just maybe—this time, I'm not meant to roll on through.

That damn smiley face on top of my name reminds me of Boone's—the one that burrows right to my insides.

I peel the foil back, and four large slices of vanilla cake with white frosting greet me. Another smile sprouts on my face. Vanilla. He remembered.

As I return to the fence, Noodles walks right up to the barrier, poking his curious nose over the top.

"That got your attention, eh?"

He nudges my shoulder, the first time he's attempted his version of a hug, and a warmth spreads through my chest. Slow and steady.

"Hang on there. You'll get yours."

I lift a piece off the plate, and the moist cake rests on my palm. I do my best to keep my fingers out of the frosting.

"Reckon this might convince you to let me climb on your back?"

It doesn't take but a second for Noodles to open his mouth and inhale the entire piece.

"No manners," I say. "I'm taking that as a yes. One more piece." I raise another, holding it just out of his reach. "Then we'll save the other two for lunch. One for you and one for me. Sound good?"

He lets out a snort, which I take as confirmation, so I feed him another piece before returning the plate to the tree and carefully covering it with the foil. Boone's smiley face beams up at me, and damn if my stomach doesn't get all stirred thinking about seeing him again.

---

AFTER DINNER, which is a mouthwatering roast beef, alongside mashed potatoes, corn on the cob, fresh bread, and a salad with more colors than a rainbow, I rush up to my room to shower and change. I don't have anything fancy, but I want to at least be clean. He's seen me in my work clothes but not my black shirt. Of all my shirts, it's the least faded. After a quick shower, I run a comb through my hair, brush my teeth, pop my hat on, grab the bunch of white clover I snatched from outside the paddock this afternoon, and mosey down to meet him.

When I poke my head into the kitchen, I don't see Boone. Or anyone. The lights are off except for a small one on the back wall. We never agreed on a meeting place, and I just assumed it would be here. My chest tightens, and I contemplate bolting up and knocking on his door, but then a small note on the stool catches my eye. It's a folded piece of paper with my name on it. Wylie. With that damn smiley face above the 'i' again.

Unfolding the message, the same handwriting meets me inside.

*Meet me at the truck. Boone.*

Before his name, he's drawn a ridiculous little heart. My mouth gets all dry, like crackling mud in the sun, and I smack my lips together, trying to gather some moisture.

Inside the first 'o' in his name he's drawn a smiley face that matches the one above mine. I wanna groan, but I'm too fucking happy.

Heading out the front, I walk past the barn, quiet now after making sure the horses were all bedded down for the night. I pause, taking an extra careful listen. Nothing. Even Dennis must be tuckered out.

The ranch pickup has been pulled out of the garage, and I spot Boone in the back, loading items into the cargo bed from his wagon. Got my first look at it with Beau, but now that I'm not working, I can fully appreciate how well maintained it is.

I'm not trying to startle Boone, so I kick my boots in the gravel a little more than I need to as I approach.

"Need help?" I ask.

Boone turns around, and my breath hitches in my throat. He's also showered, and I immediately wonder how we missed each other passing in the hallway. My dick pulses in my jeans when I picture him in the shower moments before or after me. Pondering if I'd lingered a little longer, would I have seen him in his towel? Or maybe he'd have joined me. *Easy, Wylie. Easy.*

He's got on a fancy shirt. It's plaid in all these greens that make his eyes pop like newly-shined spurs, but the buttons are a deep amber pearl, shimmering from the light outside the garage. His hat tips back, and there are more waves escaping it than I've seen before. After he drops the cooler in his arms onto the truck bed, he walks over to me.

"All set, Phyllis. But thank you."

"Pardon?"

"It's a family joke. Our great Aunt Phyllis was known for waiting until the last dish was dried and put away before asking if Ma needed any help."

"Oh. Gotcha. You should've waited for me. More than willing to load the truck," I say.

"Then none of this..." He nods at some blankets, a cooler, and another smaller bin in the bed, "would be a surprise." He motions to the passenger side. "Come on, cowboy."

"Brought you these." I hand over the clover, suddenly embarrassed at the juvenile gesture, as heat creeps over my face. "Saw them outside the paddock today and thought you might like 'em."

Boone takes the flowers, gives them a quick sniff, and says, "Mmm, take a whiff."

He holds them out, and I do as I'm told.

"They almost have a faint vanilla scent, right?" He pulls them back, taking another smell. "You know almost all the parts of white clover are edible. The flowers can be dried and used for tea. The leaves are delicious in a salad. I'm saving these."

He takes my hand and walks me to the passenger side of the truck.

"You okay letting me drive?"

He's talking about the truck, but I'm hoping he means tonight. Us. Whatever this is we're doing.

I nod and climb in, admiring the shiny, clean cab, the leather seats gleaming in the soft light spilling from the garage. Boone jogs around the front, his boots thudding against the gravel, and hops in beside me with a grin.

"Don't have the resources or time for a vehicle of my own, but gosh, when I do, this is exactly the type of ride I'd want," I say. "Mighty clean for a ranch vehicle."

"That's all Beau. This is his prized pony. He insists it's the one vehicle not covered in dust, hay, and—well, shit."

A laugh trots out of my mouth, because he's right. Everything else on the ranch has fallen to that fate.

"Good call," I reply. "Such a nice truck."

I run my hands along the leather seat beneath me, admiring the upgrades.

"He says we need at least one truck that doesn't look like a disaster for heading into town, errands, shopping. And courting."

He tosses me a wink, gives the truck's engine a turn, and we rumble off down one of the dusty dirt roads that snake through the heart of the ranch like veins through a tough old cowboy's hands.

"You do a lot of that?" I ask.

"Errands? Shopping? Try to avoid it if I can. We use what we grow and raise here on the ranch best we can. The other stuff Winnie will grab. Or Beau, when he heads into town for business. I make the lists, and they buy the stuff. Works out well for me."

That tumbling in my stomach comes back, and I take a deep breath before replying.

"No... courtin'."

"Oh gosh, no. I mean, it hasn't really been a priority. Too occupied with my family, the staff, and keeping Dennis out of the house. And most of the cowboys who come through aren't here for long. They stay for the rodeo at the beginning of the month then skedaddle."

I swallow hard, my throat dry and crackly like a ditch in a drought.

"I've had a few... admirers over the years, but nothing serious," he says.

Boone takes a right past the edge of the potato crops and into a cornfield. Never noticed the road before, and we're surrounded by tall stalks that rustle and brush against the truck's side.

"What about you?" he asks. "A different... person in every ranch?"

Is that what he thinks of me? Hitching around from place to place, staying to work and make a little money and fucking whoever is willing?

"No. Not at all. Mostly, I just... stay to myself. Most places aren't as..."

"Queer?" Boone's hand lands on my knee, sending a flash of electricity up my leg. How does he do it without worry? Yeah, we're alone in the truck in the middle of nowhere, but still. "I mean, we called it Rainbow Ranch for that reason. If you come here, you're either queer, questioning, or a fierce ally. We don't tolerate anything less."

"Yeah. That."

His fearlessness gives me a shot of bravery and without overthinking it, I move my palm to the top of his hand—the warmth of our skin touching melts any resolve I had about playing coy with Boone Adams.

"I know there are other guys out there." My thumb rubs over his rough skin until it lands on the smooth nail of his thumb. "But it never seemed worth the risk. Lots of horrible stories."

Boone nods, takes my hand up to his mouth and kisses the back of it.

"Not on our ranch." He gives my knuckles another peck. "You're safe here."

His lips brush my fingers, lingering a little longer, and Lord, my heart pounds so loudly, I'm sure he can hear it. My inclination would usually be to pull back. But we're all alone out here in the truck. It's late. We're safe.

The truck bounces over the last ridge of the cornfield, the tall stalks parting like a curtain, and suddenly, the world opens up. The engine hums quietly as the wheels roll onto soft grass, and the land stretches out into a clearing—one I've not seen or heard about in the few weeks I've been here. It's perfectly framed under the vast, open sky. Starlight spills down like liquid silver, untouched and pure.

Boone brings the truck to a stop, the quiet settling in around us. He pulls the key from the ignition with a deliberate motion, holding it for a moment before dropping it into his pocket. His eyes flick to me, and a crooked smile tugging at the corner of his mouth gives me my first glimpse of his dimple tonight.

"Ready, cowboy?"

The question hangs in the cool evening air, the kind of stillness that makes everything feel sharper.

"Yeah," I reply, my voice rougher than I intended. "Cookie."

His grin widens, teeth flashing.

"I know it's a pretty common name for ranch cooks, but no one really calls me that."

"Really?" I reach over, taking his hand and running my fingers lightly over his. "I think it suits you."

My pulse races, the excitement building like the hum of a live wire. My hands are steady on the seat, but inside, there's a heat rising, something wild and untamed. Boone doesn't wait for me to say more. He's already reaching for the door, pulling it open with a satisfying creak. The truck door slams behind him, and the night feels even more alive, like it's waiting for us to make a move.

I swing my legs out, planting my boots on the earth, and as I stand, the breeze catches my shirt, ruffling it against my skin. The stars are brilliant, their light scattered across the sky like a trail of dust. For a moment, before joining Boone, all I can do is breathe it in.

13

———

## BOONE

EVER SINCE THE first day he arrived, I've thought about bringing Wylie to my secret spot. The moment he glanced at me with those big brown eyes, lingering a second longer than I expected, I knew, when the time was right, we'd end up here. Under the big Oklahoma sky.

Rainbow Ranch is almost an hour from the closest town, and that's barely got forty thousand people. We don't create much light pollution out here, and on a clear night the sky can take your breath away. That's my hope for tonight—to steal a little of Mr. Anderson's breath.

Over the years, a few folks have referred to me as the cookie—but no one's ever used it instead of my name. Something's shifting between Wylie and me, and bringing him out here might just make it clear.

Once I'm round the back of the truck to lower the tailgate, I hear the passenger door close, and Wylie joins me. He's wearing a black shirt that almost disappears in the night. In the starlight, I can just make out his skin where it pokes through, thick arms where he's rolled it up past his elbows. His neck taunts me where he's left the top two buttons open. Even at night, he's got his hat on. A true cowboy, through and through.

"Let me," he says, moving to the bed. "You loaded. I insist."

"Nope." I climb up and move the cooler and tub toward the tailgate. "We're not unloading. Staying right here." I pat the side of the cab.

Wylie hops up, standing near the back, like a kid dragged to the doctor against his will.

"No better view for stargazing," I say.

I unfurl the first blanket into the cargo area. It's an extra I grabbed from the barn and has a few rogue pieces of hay stuck to it.

"Now this one," I say, pulling the quilt from a clean duffel, "Ma quilted this when we were kids. She took all four of us to the store in town and let each of us pick a fabric. It's become our family quilt—a little piece of each of us stitched into every square."

Smoothing out the edges, I point to the fabric I chose when Beau and I were barely nine. The print's faded now, but you can still make out the pattern—a collection of bright, hand-painted images of kitchen tools and ingredients. There's a rolling pin, a stack of flour sacks, sprigs of rosemary, and a wooden spoon. The colors are warm, like the sun-drenched afternoons we'd spend in the kitchen, rolling out dough or stirring a pot. Every time I see that pattern, it takes me back to the hours I'd spend first watching, then helping Ma cook. A small, woven piece of home, stitched into the quilt like a memory I can hold onto.

I kick off my boots, toss them onto the tailgate, and crawl toward the cab, the quilt padding my knees. I lean back against the cab, propping myself up on one elbow, and pat the spot next to me. "Come. Got a good view from here."

He follows my lead, lifting a leg up and giving his boot a hard tug. His balance shifts, his other foot sliding on the exposed horse blanket, and before I can react, he's tipping sideways.

Instinctively, I lunge toward him, my hands catching him just as he starts to lose his footing. His shoulder crashes into mine, and the force of it sends us both stumbling back. Wylie lets out a surprised grunt as we land, his torso sprawled across mine.

"Easy there, cowboy!" I try to steady us both as his weight presses into me. Wylie's laughter bursts out, a sharp, unexpected sound in the quiet of the night. For a second, we lay there, tangled up, trying to catch our breath.

"Guess I'm not as nimble as I thought," he says between chuckles.

As he clears his throat, a wide smile slowly forms on his face. His hands are still wrapped around my shoulders, but it's clear he's not going anywhere soon.

"You good?" I ask, trying to steady myself.

Wylie nods, holding on for a second longer before pulling himself up and taking a deep breath. "Yeah. Just testing my footing." His grin doesn't falter as he successfully removes his boots and shifts to sit beside me, a little more cautiously now.

I roll my eyes but let out a soft laugh. "You know, if you want to cuddle, you can just ask."

He coughs next to me, and I nudge his shoulder with mine. Something about being close, touching him out here under the stars, makes my insides settle.

"Cooler's full. Water. Tea. Threw in some of Beau's craft beers, if that tickles your fancy." I nod to the tub. "I know we already ate, but I made some snacks," I add, my voice soft, like I'm trying to hide the little bit of pride that's creeping in.

He raises an eyebrow, leaning forward, his curiosity piqued. "Snacks?"

I give a small, knowing smile and reach for the tub, pulling out a couple of bundles wrapped in wax paper. As I open one, the unmistakable scent of fresh, homemade cornbread wafts up, golden and buttery. I break off a piece and hand it over, watching as Wylie takes it with a raised brow.

"Smells like heaven," he teases, but the hint of surprise in his voice is genuine.

He takes a bite, and his expression shifts, the warmth of the cornbread softening his usual easy smirk.

"Damn," he mutters, eyes half lidded as he chews, "This is good. What else you got?"

I pull out another bundle, this time unwrapping it to reveal a batch of salted caramel popcorn, the kind that's just the right balance of sweet and savory.

"Since you've confessed to liking sweets," I say.

The scent hits the air, and Wylie leans in almost immediately, his grin returning.

"You've been holding out on me." He grabs a handful, stuffing it into his mouth with the kind of enthusiasm that only comes from a man starving for something more than just a good time. I laugh, watching the delight on his face as he munches.

The night settles around us, the quiet punctuated only by our snacking, the rustling of the corn stalks in the breeze, and my heart thumping through my shirt. I hand him a bottle of tea, watching his lips as he takes a sip.

"Maybe next time I'll bring cake," I say, settling against

the truck's cab, the stars above us twinkling like they're in on the joke.

"Cake, huh?" Wylie's voice is playful, but I'm unsure if he gets what I mean. "Now you're speaking my language."

We fall quiet, the snacks and drinks forgotten for a moment as we both lean back to watch the stars.

"Do you think Noodles will be ready for the rodeo?" I ask. "You know, there's no pressure—nobody expects miracles."

"Came awful close today," he says, his voice low and a little amused. "After two pieces of your cake, he almost let me…"

I raise an eyebrow, the thought trailing off as I glance over at him. He shifts slightly, looking over at me with that half smile of his, like he's about to let me in on some secret.

"He did?" I ask, leaning on him a bit.

Wylie grins, tapping his hand on my thigh in a slow rhythm, clearly enjoying the suspense. "I was halfway there, just about ready to swing up on his back, but then he got that look in his eye."

I chuckle, imagining the scene, the wild unpredictability of a horse challenging a seasoned rider like him. "What do you mean?"

Wylie shrugs, his grin widening. "He's not ready. Yet." He pauses, squinting into the distance, like he's still seeing it. "But he will be. Right before I made my move, he kind of side-eyed me, and I knew. We gotta build up to it. We're getting there. Just need some time."

He's talking about Noodles, I know, but a part of me thinks he might mean us, too.

"Not much time," I say, again, referring to both.

We rest our hats on the cooler and stare up. When I

spot a shooting star, I point, releasing more of my weight onto his shoulder.

"Look," I whisper, not wanting the world to hear us.

My body lingers on his, and Wylie wraps his arm around me, pulling me closer. Usually, I'd wish upon a star, but the silent joy of this moment—just him and me beneath the countless glittering stars—feels like my wish has already come true.

"C'mere." I'm a good two inches taller than him and probably weigh at least twenty pounds more, but he's doing his best to tuck me into his chest.

The fresh sweet and grassy smell of the corn settles in as we watch the sky, and a part of me wishes we could stay like this forever.

"Seems you can see the whole universe." He gazes at the sky, eyes scanning. "Thanks for bringing me out here."

I curl into him, laying my cheek on his chest, the firm muscle soothing.

The quiet night stretches around us, and the stars twinkle overhead, but it's the steady rhythm of Wylie's breathing that anchors me. His warmth seeps into my skin, and for a moment, everything else fades into the background, leaving only the stars and the quiet hum of his breath.

"We should probably head back soon," I say. "We've both got to be up early."

He lets out a deep exhale, his breath hitting my hair as he wraps his other arm around me, squeezing me tight.

"Only take me a minute to clean up."

The cooler and tub are open, and there's a few plates and bottles in the cab.

"Before I put all this away, want anything else?"

I sit up, and Wylie's hands move to my shoulders. He's staring at me, his eyes catching the light from the stars.

"Yeah."

He moves a hand to my chin, holding me in place.

"You."

There's no sweet, soft kiss on the cheek this time. Wylie pulls me close, our faces near enough that the cornbread and popcorn on his breath reaches my nose.

"Happy to oblige," I say.

He captures my lips, enveloping me in his arms and leaning back against the cab. As my tongue tangles with his, we scoot down, so I'm on top of him. Even though I'm bigger, he supports my weight easily, guiding me down so my entire body rests on his. His right hand reaches for my face, brushing a thumb across my cheek, playing in my dimple. I've got a hand on his chest, but he grabs the other, weaving our fingers together like plaits of bread eager to be braided.

"So damn sweet," he says, pausing the kiss. "Like cake."

I chuckle and say, "You're becoming more and more fond of sweets."

"These." He touches my lips, gliding his finger across them. "Yeah."

His mouth returns to kissing, soft moans from both of us filling the quiet night air.

Holding his chest and hand while our tongues wrestle gives me the courage to take a nip at his lower lip, tugging and pulling softly. This elicits a deeper gravely groan from him and sends a jolt of excitement to my groin.

"I'm not crushing you, am I?" I ask, lifting my torso off him.

This has the unplanned effect of smashing our lower

halves together, and apparently all the kissing has turned Wylie on as much as me.

"Cookie," he mutters, and heat flushes through my chest, crawling up my neck. "You're good. Great."

He pulls me down, and his hands migrate to my back before crawling down to my ass. He's tentative, lingering near my belt, before I nod. "Please."

Wylie shoves his hands into my pants and under my underwear. He cups my cheeks, squeezing, and then hauls me closer, our boners smashing against each other through layers of fabric.

"I'm so fucking hard." He dips his head and hides his eyes.

I reach for his chin, lifting his gaze to meet mine.

"Me, too."

I thrust my cock on his, holding his face in place, our foreheads touching as I steal another bite at his lower lip.

"Should we..." His voice is barely audible. "Go somewhere?"

"Nowhere more private than here," I say. "Maybe a few owls. Bats. That's it."

"Don't mind either." Wylie's breath tickles my face.

He dips in for another kiss, pulling my hips firm.

"They both do a good job of clearing out the pests."

"You sure?" I ask. "Not about the critters." I rut into him, my dick longing to be free. "'Bout this. Cause, I'm sure. Surer than sure."

He nods, and I'm up, tugging at my belt, trying to undress as quickly as possible. He just watches, a smirk tugging at his mouth as I yank my pants and underwear down to my knees in one swoop.

"Boone, I should warn ya..."

Crap. Here it comes. He's actually straight. Married.

Has a family in Albuquerque. On the run. A fugitive. Wanted in four states for bank robbery. This is why I shouldn't waste my time on sexy cowboys. Fuck, what have I gone and gotten myself into?

"It's been a while." He dips his chin again, and now, with my cock at full attention, I move next to him.

"Same," I say. "There's no pressure."

I move to pull my pants up.

"No," he says. "Just not sure what you're expecting... not going to take long is all."

"Oh," I say as it registers. "Mr. Anderson, I'm good with that."

I move my hand to my hard dick, waiting.

"We could get each other off," I say, stroking slowly.

"Maybe I could kiss you while we do it?" he asks. "Or not. Just an idea."

A thrilling buzz, like a thousand bees, vibrates through every inch of my body.

"Yeah," I say. "I'd like that."

I'm up, kneeling, reaching for his belt, unbuckling as my lips find his. Luckily, all the kneading and rolling in the kitchen has made my fingers strong, and I'm able to get it open without looking. I'm over him, his tongue swirling in my mouth as I undo the button of his jeans. His warm fingers wrap around my cock, holding me at first, and then running his hand down the shaft to my balls. He cups them, running a finger underneath, locking his eyes with mine. The sensation—just a little pressure—makes my cock harder, and I nod.

"Oh, fuck, yeah," I murmur.

When I've got him unbuttoned and unzipped, Wylie lifts his hips so I can slide his jeans down to his thighs. It's enough. For now. My eyes are fixated on his face as we kiss, but my fingers get the first impression of him.

His dick is long. Definitely longer than mine. What is it about men instantly comparing cocks? Guess it's in our DNA. Pretty sure mine is thicker, but there's more than enough there to make me smile into his kiss. He's stone solid, and when my fingers skate over the head, he's leaking precum. Based on what he said, I suspect it won't take very long. We're both about to explode, but I want just a little more.

I'm on my knees, our mouths never parting, while we jerk each other off. And even though it's late, and we both need to be up early, I don't want it to end. Or at least, not like this.

Breaking the kiss, I move back to catch my breath. He's leaning against the cab, his raging boner resting on his furry stomach. My eyes have adjusted to the darkness, and the stars provide enough light for me to take him all in. His thick bush melts into the light fur on his belly, and I need to open that shirt. Soon. He's completely vulnerable like this, but I'm a gentleman.

"You're close," I say.

He nods. "Yup. Might pop just from staring at you."

My pants have fallen to my ankles, and I'm on all fours, ass up, hard cock pointing down.

Moving on him, I press my lips to his, reaching down to grip him. After another kiss, I lean back and whisper, "Wanna come in my mouth?"

"Oh fuck, Cookie." He blows out a long breath, his lips forming a perfect O, as a smile plays on my lips while he gently cups my chin.

"Soon." I glide my thumb over the slick head of his cock,

and he lets out a soft moan. He's so close. "I want your cock inside me. Mine inside you."

He gives a single nod, and I rest my forehead on his. I'm holding his dick, but I don't dare stroke him for fear he'll erupt before I get my lips around him.

Starting with a kiss on his nose, I continue down to his lips and chin, then plant soft kisses on his neck while unbuttoning his shirt. I open the rest, and his pecs, firm and covered in soft brown hair the same color as his head, greet me. As I press my lips on them, I make a silent promise to give them more attention next time.

When my mouth lands on his stomach, inches from my target, he lets out a small laugh. Another mental note. *He's ticklish.* I'll have fun with this next time, too.

"Ready," I say into his stomach, eliciting more chuckles.

He doesn't reply, but when I look up, he clasps my chin and runs his finger over my lips again, staring intently as he nods.

With permission granted, I take in the head, savoring the salty, sticky liquid as it coats my tongue—signaling that, yeah, this won't take long.

With soft moans that fill the night air, he grabs the sides of my head, hands getting lost in my hair as he holds on. I swallow more of him, doing my best to open the back of my throat. It's been a few years, but thankfully, like making an old favorite dish, it all comes flooding back.

With a few long sucks, Wylie thrusts up, fucking into my mouth, and the faint gagging noises from my throat mix with his heavy breathing and the chirping of insects in the distance.

With heavy pants escaping his mouth, I reach down, massaging his balls. They contract in my hand as Wylie gasps, and his cock throbs in my mouth, shooting warm cum down the back of my throat. He lifts his hips higher, shaking, moaning, and spurring me on. I swallow as much as possible as he continues firing into me—but there's too much, and it dribbles down my chin.

Wylie swipes it with his thumb, and I open my mouth, inviting him to pop it in. Even after swallowing the remnants of his load, I can't help but keep his finger in my mouth a moment longer, relishing the lingering taste of him.

When he finishes, his bare ass resting on our family quilt, I gobble him back down because it was too quick. He's still hard, and I crave more.

"Boone, Boone. Damn, Cookie."

With my lips still stretched around him, I glance up and look into his eyes.

"You're fucking beautiful." His fingers caress my cheeks, and when I give another good draw on his dick before pulling off, his hips shudder.

"I'm close," I say.

Wylie stares at me, his forehead wrinkling.

"Kiss me," I say. "Please."

He tugs my shirt, pulling me up and capturing my lips as I stroke myself. The build-up from the last few days intensifies as the muscles in my body tighten. My breath quickens. I'm huffing into his mouth, but he doesn't seem to mind. He reaches down, and I'm about to let go, allowing him to take over, but he doesn't grab my dick. His hand moves under me, pawing at my bare ass, fingers poking at my hole. Yeah, I'm about to pop.

"Fuck, cowboy." I spill the words into his mouth. "You're making me come."

My dick unloads, sending thick bands of cum onto Wylie's hairy chest. The moment it happens, I realize what a mess it's going to be, but I can't stop. Won't stop. His fingers linger on my hole, applying pressure around the perimeter, enjoying every contraction as I coat his torso.

When I'm done and breathless, I settle next to him, both our cocks still out. He's soft now, and mine is on its way.

"Damn, I'm sorry. You're a mess," I say, surveying my handiwork.

"Get over here." He pulls my chin toward him, kissing my lips softly.

"This—" he nods to his exposed chest and stomach, "—is perfect."

The sweet taste of his lips lingers as his breath mingles with mine, and a wave of warmth washes over me. We need to clean up, but in this moment, sprawled half naked beneath the starlit sky, everything feels exactly as it should. Nothing else matters but us.

14

———

WYLIE

SPENDING time with Boone in the back of the truck, under the stars, did something to me. Yeah, I got my rocks off in a way I haven't in a very long time, but it wasn't only that. It scratched something deep inside. Something not used to being scratched—my dang heart.

The few times I've been with other men, it was always quick. Dirty. In a tent up on a mountain corralling sheep. Behind a barn after mucking out the stalls. Never much talking and rarely kissing. And if there was, it wasn't... sweet. Caring. All the things Boone makes me feel when he looks at me with those giant green eyes. Like he's cooking something up in that head of his.

Over the next few days, we fall into a rhythm. It's new for me, but I try not to overthink it. Kinda like riding off a cliff, but knowing someone will catch you—that's what he does to me.

I see him at breakfast every day. The first morning after the night under the stars, I snuck in early for a kiss. But when Boone brought out biscuits slathered in gravy, he placed the platter on the table then slathered me with his own kiss. Right in front of the entire crew seated around the table. Beau gave me a wink, but otherwise, nobody said boo about it.

Tonight, when Boone brings out a large bowl of salad, he places it in the center of the table with a flourish.

"White clover," he says and shoots me a wink.

Sure enough, atop the salad, scattered like tiny emerald confetti, are the leaves from the flowers I gave him.

"Seriously? You're putting weeds in the salad now?" Benny teases.

Boone just grins, laying a hand on my shoulder. "They're not weeds; they're wild *herbs*—good for you, and taste better than you'd think." He gives me a tap.

Benny grabs a sprig, pops it into his mouth, and gives a faint nod.

"Okay, okay. Not horrible," he admits, still chewing.

"See?" Boone leans forward, his stomach against my upper back. "Nature's little gifts. You just have to know where to get 'em."

He squeezes my shoulders, now with both hands, then heads back into the kitchen.

After dinner, I give Boone space to do what he needs in the kitchen and spend more time with Noodles. I sit in his stall with him and bring him that cake Boone bakes especially for me to feed him—always vanilla with less sugar in the icing. We're not trying to have a sick horse on our hands.

I talk to Noodles, more than I've talked to almost anyone. I take time to tell him about my family. The good times, before it all went to crap. He swishes his tail, usually falling asleep standing up, but I know he hears me. Noodles doesn't judge. Talking to him might be good practice for saying it all to someone else someday.

It feels good to get it out, like a rope deep inside me that's been tangled in knots finally coming free.

After Boone finishes in the kitchen, I hear him take the trash and compost out, and I head over to meet him. We walk on the dirt road that leads to the spot he took me to in the truck, occasionally stopping to lock lips. Sometimes we get a little handsy, but mostly it's just kissing.

On Saturday, Boone takes me out past the cornfields where the stars work overtime to shine through the clouds. After my lips are red and swollen from being kissed, sucked, and bitten, we rest on the ground, surrounded by the tall stalks. There's a spark deep in my chest—flickering at first, then growing to a steady burn—and for once, I don't keep it in. I say something first.

"You don't mind?"

"Mind what?"

Boone's between my legs, laying back on my chest. My arms wrap around his torso as we stare into the sky, searching.

"Only kissing?"

Before he can answer, a tinge of worry flickers in my stomach. Maybe he didn't enjoy the night in the truck. Had I done something wrong?

I grind my teeth and pull Boone closer. He's here with me, and has been every night since then.

"Are you kidding me?"

He sits up, shifting so he's looking at me, the same way he was staring at the sky.

"I love kissing you."

As if to prove it, he ghosts his lips on mine and lingers a little.

"I wasn't trying to pressure you." Boone's breath tickles

my nose. "For more. I know you're not staying much past the rodeo."

I take a deep breath, focusing on his face, trying to get it out.

"What if..."

In the moonlight, Boone's eyes search mine for more. I gaze at his beautiful face. His beautiful soul. I don't want to quit him. The words tumble out before I can stop them.

"What if I stayed?"

He's quiet. His perfect lips part, but only air escapes.

"Have to talk to Beau, of course. Wouldn't want to overstay my welcome. But Noodles and I seem to have a good thing going. Wouldn't want him to pull back into his shell after I left."

A smile tugs at his lips, like he's trying to keep it at bay.

"I mean, we can't upset Noodles," he says. "And if you want me to talk to Beau, say the word. He doesn't want folks to know it, but he's a softy. Okay, not really. But for me, yes. He may only be two minutes older, but I'll always be his baby brother."

I shake my head. "Thanks, but I'll talk to him. Still got a week to get Noodles in shape. Kinda want to make a little more progress first."

"Totally understandable. Now, back to the kissing." He dips in and steals one. "I'm in no rush, but I wouldn't mind a repeat of the other night, either."

"Ain't got no truck," I say, glancing around.

"No, but we both have rooms."

"That allowed?" I ask. "Not trying to break any rules before I have a chat with the boss about staying on."

"It's allowed, so long as we're not disturbing anyone. Trust me, my siblings have plenty of fun in their quarters."

He lets out a big yawn that goes on and on, and I quickly realize he's faking it.

"Boy, am I tired." He wrangles up another bogus yawn. "Best be getting back... to our rooms."

With a flush of heat to my neck, I push myself to stand, grabbing his hand and yanking him up after me.

"Better get back, then."

I give his ass a quick slap with my free hand, and we head back. Before I know it, our pace quickens, and we start to jog, with quiet laughter between us and the cool night air rushing against our faces. All that exists is the beat of our feet, a primal rhythm against the earth, and the magnetic pull of the main house drawing us closer.

## 15

## BOONE

WE STUMBLE UP THE STAIRS, drunk on excitement. It's been a few days since we got our rocks off in the truck, and I'm really hoping we both last longer this time. When our laughter becomes a little too loud for the late hour, I pause midway up the stairs and give Wylie my best stern look. The one Ma used to give us when we got caught stealing cookies out of the jar before bedtime.

Wylie's brows raise, betraying a flash of guilt as a half-formed smile hangs on the corner of his lips. Dear Lord, he's handsome enough to eat—which is exactly my plan.

When we're at the top of the stairs, near the first bathroom, I pause and lean in to whisper in his ear.

"My room. Fifteen minutes."

When his eyes register confusion, I say, "I'm jumping in the shower." I nod toward my room and the other bathroom at the far end of the hall. "Lickety-split, I promise."

After the quickest shower of my life, making sure all my important bits are squeaky clean, I close the bathroom door as quietly as possible, and tip-toe the six feet to my room.

The moment I step in front of Billie's door, the floorboard creaks, and it pops open.

"Abilene," I say, tipping an imaginary hat.

"You're out late."

We don't keep tabs on each other like that, so I know she's only sassing me.

"Just out stargazing."

I smile, gripping the towel around my waist as water drips from my hair onto my forehead.

"Needed a shower after?"

She dips her chin and cocks her head, looking so much like Ma it hurts.

"Wanna be clean for bed."

"Mmm hmm. For bed. And it wouldn't have anything to do with a certain cowboy I saw sneaking into your room a few minutes ago?"

"Night, Billie."

I lean over and give her a quick kiss on the forehead.

"You're wet!" She pulls away, retreating into her room.

With a smirk on my face, I stand at my door, clutching the towel in place. I enter in one swift motion, closing the door behind me, taking a moment to catch my breath before turning around. When I do, my eyes almost pop out of my head when I take in the sight waiting for me.

Wylie's lounging on my bed, propped up on his hands. He's completely naked except for his weathered cowboy hat and the boots hugging his feet. A shudder of pleasure rips through me, and even though I'm only wearing a towel, I'm suddenly extremely warm. I adore cooking, but maybe I should've been a painter.

"Howdy, partner," I say with a lick of my lips.

Getting my first look at him naked, excitement ripples

through my body. He's fucking delicious. With my bedside lamp on, I'm able to see him much clearer than the night on the truck. The hair on his chest is darker than on his head, but there's not as much as I thought I saw under only starlight. His nipples poke through it, and my mouth waters thinking about what I might do with them.

"Boots and hat?" I ask.

Wylie holds his cock up, hard and pointing right at me. Hopefully, a promise.

"Happy to remove them. Just thought you might..."

I remove my towel, my dick already almost matching his hardness.

"No, leave 'em for now," I say. "Save a horse."

He laughs, a booming sound that shakes his shoulders and tilts his head back. His Adam's apple bobs with each chuckle. "You wanna ride a cowboy?"

"Something like that." I toss my towel on the floor, and kneel before him. "First, I wanna taste him."

With my face only inches from his groin, I rest my hands on his thighs, taking in his musky aroma. His day of working with the horses, then out in the paddock—he smells like hay and sunshine, and I'm eager to savor him again.

While Wylie jerks his dick, I place my hand over his, getting swept along in the moment.

"Easy, buddy," I say. "I want us to last longer this time."

He laughs. "Me too. C'mere, first."

His hands scoop under my arms, lifting me so I'm kneeling between his legs, still gripping his cock as he dips down and captures my lips with his. The sweetness lasts about five seconds before Wylie's tongue juts in. I push his hat back, giving us more room, his stubble causing the finest friction on my face. He's moaning softly and my cock stiffens with each sound. His hands land on my chest, pinching at both of my nipples as I slide my thumb back and forth over the tip of his dick.

I stroke him, and his fingers flick and massage my chest, sending another shudder of pleasure zooming to my cock, which rubs against his shin as I grind into him.

"Dang, Cookie." There's gravel in his voice as he pulls back and leans back on his elbows again.

I raise my eyebrows and apply a firmer grip to his cock, its heat and hardness beneath my fingertips. Our breaths quicken, and I'm eager to devour him.

He sits back on my bed with his arms flexed, and I notice the sheen of sweat on his forehead under his hat. I crawl up, my hands next to his body, until my mouth lands on his chin. I plant a soft kiss and nibble on his lower lip as our erections smash together between us.

"Fuck, I wanna suck you."

His dick, yeah—but all of him. My tongue glides down his neck, taking in the sweet ripeness of his day. When I reach his chest, my mouth takes a nipple in, biting lightly. I'm careful not to hurt him, but he grunts, the vibration from his throat evident.

"So damn sexy." I take a quick lick at his pec. "And tasty."

My hand glides down to cup his balls. I add some pressure right underneath as I pepper his stomach with kisses. He squirms a little when I suck on his belly. I peek up at him, and he's tipped his hat down to cover his face. A smirk skates across my face knowing I'm tickling him.

"Now," I say, taking his cock with both hands. "You tell me if you get close, because I have some other things in mind."

"Okay." He's moved his hat back, and he's watching me now. "Should be good for a spell."

He winks and heat rumbles in my core. My cock throbs, and I swallow him as far as I'm able. When my nose brushes the soft hair at the base of his dick, and Wylie's body melts under me, I know he's enjoying himself.

"That first night I arrived..." His voice catches me off guard, and I pause with my tongue resting on the tip. "Don't stop," he begs. "Please."

He continues talking, and I resume guzzling.

"I was in my room. Watching you."

I run my lips up and down his shaft, my tongue taking a swipe at his hairy balls. He smells like heaven.

"You were taking the trash out. Bent over. Your ass in those jeans—fucking perfect. Got me so damn hard. I stared at you while I jerked off."

Pulling off, I lift my head to look at him—a bead of saliva tethering Wylie's cock to my lips.

He slaps it against my cheek, eliciting a smile from me as he shoves the head of his cock into my dimple. Nobody's ever done that. It's amazing. I lean into it, spit and precum enhancing the sensation.

"I've wanted you." He sighs. "Since then."

My body is torn between the pressing need to finish the task and the irresistible urge to kiss him.

I wipe my mouth with the back of my palm and catch my breath. Wylie sits up, his calloused hands lifting me to stand between his legs.

My boner points straight ahead, and he grasps my hips, pulling me closer. He lowers his head, his hat shielding my view, and then Wylie Anderson's lips, plump from kissing, latch onto me.

The muscles in my midsection contract, his warm mouth drawing me in. A rush of sensation courses through my body, my eyes rolling back as I savor every moment. He moves off, licking the tip, and I reach down and tilt his hat more, his stubbly chin coming into view. When he attempts to take me all the way in, his hat bumps my body, and he pulls off, gagging.

"Take it easy, cowboy," I say. "Don't hurt yourself."

"That's one fuckin' fat cock." He looks up at me, licking his lips.

"You like it?" I rub the head against his wet mouth.

"Almost as much as your cake."

I'm not sure if he's talking about my sheet cake or my ass, but I don't ask. "Swallow it, then."

I thrust back into his mouth, my dick disappearing as he relaxes his jaw, taking me deeper. There's still small choking noises, but when Wylie reaches down and strokes himself, I figure he's more than okay.

Gasping for air, he pulls back, slapping my cock against his stubbly cheek, sending a shiver up my spine. I lean down for a kiss, and his lips, swollen from the intensity of kissing and sucking, make me want to push him back on the bed and climb right on top of him.

Taking a breath, Wylie reaches around my waist, his hands landing on my ass.

"That night, I watched you. All I could think about was getting up in here."

He's holding my cheeks open, patting a finger near my hole, poking and exploring. I lower myself, nodding slowly, urging him on.

He stands, the worn leather of his boots creaking softly on the wood floor as he moves behind me, wrapping his arm around my chest and kissing the back of my neck.

Barely above a whisper, Wylie's warm breath tickles my ear. "Lay on the bed."

I turn around and lay back, but he interrupts me.

"On your belly."

My eyes widen, and I flip over.

"How's that?"

I glance back, and he's tipped his hat so far back I expect it to fall.

He kneels over me, spreading my ass again with his hands, and I arch my back.

"Wondered if you had any ink," he says.

"It's the ranch tattoo. We all have it. You gotta search a little to find mine."

"It's fuckin hot." He traces the horseshoe on my right cheek with a finger. "Get that ass up for me."

I grab my pillow and bury my face in it while he moves back, his fingers never leaving my body, until it happens. He kisses both cheeks, pulls me as far apart as he can, and his tongue skates around the perimeter.

I do the best to muffle my moans, but when Wylie's mouth covers my entire opening and his tongue juts in, I'm not sure all the pillows on the ranch can contain the noise that comes out of me.

He pulls back, his warm breath on my ass as he whispers, "Arch your back."

I do as I'm told, and he's able to plunge even deeper. I'm able to reach under and stroke myself while he makes a feast out of me. He pulls out, and gives my ass a loud slap.

"Better than any dessert." Wylie's breath makes every nerve in my ass come alive. "Gettin' you nice and ready."

He's playing with me. Fucking me with a finger, his thumb I think. Shaking my ass with wide, palmed hands.

Licking. Jutting his tongue back in. Staring at my butt jiggling under his touch.

"Boone?" He doesn't take his hands off me.

I lift my head. "Yeah?"

"You wanna get fucked?"

Every nerve in my body catches fire. Finally. Thank God.

HEAVEN. Sure, all the stealing kisses and cuddling in the cornfields has been amazing, but this—being naked with Boone Adams in the privacy of his room—takes it to a whole new level. His skin on mine. His mouth on mine. And that ass. I'm a coiled spring. The need to be near him is a physical ache, a vibration that runs from my hat to my boots.

I haven't had another guy's dick in my mouth in... years. Only once. Just hasn't happened since then, and now all I want is to taste him. His dick. His skin. His mouth. His ass.

He's not as hairy as me, but there's a little dusting of fuzz on his butt—like the softest peach—and my cock throbs as I touch it. When I slap his horseshoe tattoo, it jiggles, and I sure hope it does that when I'm railing him—shakes like jello as I pump into him.

"Got any condoms?" I ask. "I should've thought of that. Honestly, haven't been to a store since I got here, and I'm... if you don't, we can just..."

"Hold on," Boone says, reaching for the bedside table.

He pulls a wrapped condom and a small tube from the drawer, his face breaking into a wide, eager smile.

"Beau buys 'em in bulk."

He shrugs and hands me the rubber. The lube opens with a loud click, and he begins applying it to himself.

"I was tested last year when we all went to Tulsa for physicals." Boone squirts more into his palm and reaches around to get himself ready. "Haven't been with anyone since."

"No other cowboys traveling through?"

My hands focus on rolling the condom over my dick, pulling it down, avoiding the pebble in my gut thinking about Boone with other men.

"Wylie Anderson." He's next to me on the bed on his knees, but he drops the lube and takes my chin between his thumb and index finger.

A flutter churns in my stomach, swirling that damn stone, as I hold my breath.

"I may be friendly. I may be a flirt, but no. Actually..." He picks up the tube and applies a good amount to his palm. "I was holding out for a surly one."

He applies lube to my cock, sending a shiver through my core and then leans over, pressing his lips on mine, spreading the slickness over my dick, while his tongue runs over my teeth.

"Now, cowboy, lie back." Boone presses gently on my shoulders, guiding me to recline. Before I do, I take off my hat and set it on the bedside table, then ease back onto the pillow.

"I'm going to get things started, then you can take over." He flashes a grin so damn sexy I nearly lose control and pull him in for a kiss.

Instead of rushing to it, he straddles me, bends over, and buries his nose in my neck. Fuck, I probably should've showered when he did. I was trying to hurry and be in his room before he got back.

"Divine," he purrs into my collarbone.

Every nerve in my torso lights up like the night sky on the Fourth of July.

And then he's at my pit, running his tongue along my skin, hair, not caring a bit about the sweat from the day or since I've been in his room, my engine running hot.

He holds my arm in place, licking up to my elbow and back to my pec like a thirsty horse at a creek. It tickles a little, but it's also making my dick more solid than a mountain.

"You like that?" I ask, pretty sure of the answer by the way he's inhaling with his entire face.

He moves to the other side, repeating the attention given, and I grab onto the back of his head, letting my fingers get lost in his hair. There's something in my boot. A piece of dirt or hay, brushing against the bottom of my foot, and between that and Boone's face buried in my armpit, I'm coming undone.

When his mouth lands on my chin, biting at me like a bull snapping at the reins, my cock lifts off my stomach, aching for contact.

"Boone…" I whisper.

"Steady, cowboy. I gotcha."

His mouth moves down the center of my neck, licking, sucking, kissing every inch of me. I take a deep breath to steady myself, the pleasure already spreading like an out of control wildfire. He's leaning over, moving my dick to his desired target, and my heart thumps in my chest, watching him.

"Do you know how fucking beautiful you are?"

The words slip out and my jaw tightens. Eyes slamming shut. Meaning every word but wishing I could take it back.

"You're just saying that because you're about to fuck me." He's got me right at his hole, gliding my cock back and forth.

"True, but that's not it. You're..."

He lowers his hips, and carefully, slow like a stream after the first drops of rain, I glide inside.

"Perfect," I say, barely above a whisper. "So fucking tight."

"Yeah, well, I told ya—been awhile."

Boone takes a deep breath, and then he's still. He waits with my dick inside him all the way, his chest expanding with each breath, stomach jutting out enough to catch my gaze. There's some heft to him. He's solid, like an oak barrel —not too lean, but with enough muscle to show he's using every part of himself in that kitchen.

He lets out a long, slow breath between his perfectly pursed lips. "Now, let's see about riding you, cowboy."

With his hands now on my chest, he moves forward— just enough to leave the head inside—before pushing back. He's tentative the first few times, and when I pop out of him, he doesn't flinch. Boone moves a hand back, placing me back inside him and brushing down my cock until his fingers sweep over my balls, giving them a massage. A groan tumbles out of my mouth, the pressure in that perfect spot thrusting my hips up.

"You ready to take a turn?" There's a smirk on Boone's face that makes me smile.

I nod.

"But first..." I curl my finger, beckoning him closer.

He leans in, his lips grazing mine in a soft, fleeting kiss.

Quickly, I reach for my hat, lifting it from the bedside table and settling it gently on Boone's head.

This draws a playful grin across his lips.

"Ready, cowboy?" I ask.

"Giddy-fucking-up."

He takes a nibble at my lower lip before moving back. I move my hands to his hips, holding him place, while I fuck up, plunging myself in and out of him. He's moved a hand to his dick, not stroking, but holding himself steady.

Watching him ride me while wearing my hat, his eyes half closed, is a fucking sight. When I see his thumb making small circles over the head of his cock, slippery with precum, I grab his hand and bring it to my mouth. He pushes his thumb between my lips, the tangy flavor filling my mouth as I suck.

The harder I thrust into him, the wider Boone's smile grows. There's a complete look of contentment painted on his face as he holds onto one of my pecs while I slurp on his thumb.

"Okay, give me a sec." He rolls off and lies next to me. My hat tips off his head, and he catches it before it falls.

He hops off the bed, standing with my hat. "Let's keep this safe."

Moving to the closet, Boone holds my hat carefully, as if it's something more than just a piece of worn leather. With a quiet smile, he hangs it on the hook inside the door, the brim resting perfectly, almost reverently, against the wood. He steps back, eyes lingering on it for a moment, then turns to face me.

"Figured it deserves a good spot."

I watch him for a beat, his round ass, swaying with each step, making my heart skip. "You're something else, you know that?"

He shrugs, the smirk returning to his lips. "Just trying to take care of it."

Then, without missing a beat, he returns to the edge of the bed and sits. Before I can speak, he's stroking me.

"Plus, that gave me a break." He grabs the lube and applies more to both of us.

"Cookie, take all the time you need."

My breathing regulates a little as we rest. Boone lies next to me, rolls on his side, and kisses my cheek. When he moves to my ear, my cock surges in his grip, becoming even harder from wanting to be back inside him.

"'Bout ready to go again," I say, his fingers tapping playfully on my erection.

His lips skip across the skin behind my ear, making my insides boil like a pot of coffee on a campfire—ready to spill over any second.

"Fuck me by the window. Where you watched me," he says.

My eyebrows fly up, trying to hide. Boone's up, leaning by the open window on the opposite wall, shaking his ass at me. The curtain stirs a bit, caught by the cool night breeze. He widens his stance and turns his head to face me.

"Well?" He smiles slowly, like the sun hitting the horizon at dusk, all warm and dangerous, with enough mischief to make me wonder what trouble he's got in mind.

He turns back around, arms crossed on the sill, his juicy ass waiting.

Quick as a wink, I'm up, doing my best to keep my boots quiet as I take my place behind him. My hands climb to his shoulders, right arm wrapping around him and landing on his chest, squeezing the meaty muscle as my dick pushes against his ass.

"Fuck, you're better than a rainstorm after a drought."

He moves my hand to his cock, slick with lube and precum. "'Bout as wet too."

"You ready?" I move my hand to his chest, tugging him back.

He reaches back, spreading himself wide. With a little adjusting, my dick finds its target. Already open and ready from before, I slide right in and my shoulders drop at the solace of being inside him again.

"Cookie, you good?"

"Darn tootin'."

I laugh, because he's so fucking precious.

He pushes back, and I bend over him, matching the curve of his back with my body. I may be a couple inches shorter, but we fit like two parts of a well-oiled bridle, snug and seamless.

Our heads poke out of the curtain, the pitch black night sky greeting us as I nestle into the crook of his neck. It's well past midnight, and the moon's high, painting the ranch in silver shadows. Dark shapes of the buildings and fence posts are barely visible against the star-covered sky. The distant lowing of a cow echoes, but everything else is silent. I love this time of year. Once the sun disappears, the air becomes cool, crisp, and carries the faint scent of the barn. It's like time stands still, as Boone waits for me to pick up where we left off.

His skin smells like pine from the soap in the shower, and I take him in, kissing his neck, then the spot right between his shoulder blades as I move my hands to his waist.

"You like my cock inside you?"

I keep my voice low. Ain't nobody out at this hour, but I'm not looking to stir up any trouble or wake the dead.

He nods, and a deep *mmmh* comes from his throat as he

pushes back. I take his hint and thrust into him, pulling myself out most of the way before plunging back. We find our pace, like a colt getting used to the saddle, and my right hand, trembling slightly, finds its way back to Boone's chest.

"Fuck my hole, cowboy." His voice is lower, full of grit. "It's yours."

The warmth of his skin comforts my palm. When I drive deeper into him, he moans, probably a little louder than either of us expected, and shoves three of my fingers into his mouth.

My thumb runs up and down his cheek, until I find his dimple—a satisfied smile spreading across my lips. Boone quietly emits little grunts as I rail him by the window. The press of his bare feet against my boots sends a jolt through me. This might be more thrilling than the wildest gallop across an open field, the friction of his ass against me as he bucks back.

I come to a halt, and he takes over, giving me the chance to simply watch as my dick moves in and out, stretching his opening.

His ass gripping my cock.

His mouth sucking my fingers.

My free hand gives his butt another slap, the cheek shaking as he continues crashing back on me. The pleasure is unlike anything I've ever experienced. This isn't just two men fucking. This is two people becoming one. It's intoxicating. All-consuming. Truly awesome.

"Fuck, Cookie. You want more?"

My lips nip at his ear as he shoves back. With my fingers in his mouth, all he can manage is a moan in response.

"I'm gonna come." I spill on his earlobe. "Hard."

He makes a noise, but I can't understand, and I need to

know. With a jolt, I pull my fingers out—they're wet and sloppy.

"Inside me. I wanna feel it."

The words flow out of him like a prayer as he drives back faster, a fiery energy radiating from his powerful frame as he devours my fingers again. Then that feeling, like the earth is about to crack open, swallowing everything up, including my soul, starts in my boots, and my free hand lands on his shoulder, holding him in place while he fucks my cock.

"Holy shit," I manage to stammer out. "Keep going. Just like that. Don't stop."

He does as I say, my balls tightening, his head moving forward slightly, causing me to pull back in his mouth. He moans, louder than before, as I shoot, filling the condom while his hole clenches around me.

Connected to him this way, unloading inside him, a surge of pleasure washes over me with each blast. My torso shakes with the intense gratification of the release, and I fall onto Boone, letting my weight rest on his damp back. Even in the cool night air, we've both worked up a sweat.

My fingers trace the contours of his chest, once again pulling him close.

"I wanna stay inside you like this..." I kiss the back of his neck, the sweetness of him coating my lips. "Forever."

Boone takes a deep breath, his chest rising under my arms, and then turns around.

"That was wild." His gaze finds mine. "In the best possible way."

"What about you?" I palm his cock—he's hard and precum dribbles on my fingers.

A mischievous smile overtakes his face, and I know I'm in for a surprise. Boone Adams seems to be full of them.

"Lie down," he says.

Before I can move, he tugs the condom off my still sensitive cock. It's full, and he ties off the end and tosses it into a small wicker waste basket by the door.

I lie back with my legs hanging off the bed and prop myself on my elbows. Quick as a wink, Boone's on me, crawling over me until his mouth meets mine. My hand reaches for his neck, dragging him close, as he strokes himself over me.

He pauses the kiss, pulling back so our lips are still touching. "Won't take me long. Just want to give you a little present."

Boone's tongue pokes between my lips, and I grasp his face with both hands. The sound of him jerking his cock, slippery from the lube, and his small grunts fill the small room. When his breathing picks up, blowing into my mouth as we kiss, I move my hands to his chest, pinching his nipples.

"Okay, okay," he moans. "You ready for my load, cowboy?"

I'm speechless. So I nod, because yeah, of course I want it. Him. All of it.

Boone lowers his head, watching himself for a moment. When he starts shaking, he presses his mouth against mine. And then it hits me like a can of pop, shaken and finally opened—hot cum splatters across my chin.

With a massive grin, I respond, "Oh fuck yeah."

Boone moans over me, another eruption landing on my face.

"Damn, boy. Cover me with it."

The next few blasts hit my chest, then my stomach, and finally, my dick, already plumping again, responding to the intense heat of the moment.

He collapses next to me, burying his face in my neck.

"That was flippin' hot." I press my palm against his head, splaying my fingers through his damp hair, drawing him near.

He's still and silent.

"Cookie, you okay?"

"Mmmmh." His lips vibrate against my skin. "Can't move."

"No need to," I say, pulling him closer. "C'mere."

He casually lifts a leg over my midsection and drapes an arm over my chest. I'm a complete mess, plastered in his cum, but he doesn't seem to mind one bit.

Laying here, the cool breeze whispering through the window, I close my eyes. With a slow, steady breath, I try to take it all in—Boone beside me, the warmth in my chest, the quiet peace that's settled over us like the fields after a downpour. Ain't often I feel this way, but tonight, with him, I soak it all in.

# 17

## BOONE

THE NEXT FEW DAYS, my feet barely touch the ground as I move around the kitchen. It's like I'm floating, untethered, as if every step I take is lighter than air. My hat's the only thing keeping me from drifting away. There's this incredible sense of joy and possibility, making even the simplest tasks feel like a celebration. When I stir a pot, chop vegetables, or flip sizzling bacon, it's like I'm doing it all in a dream, carried along by a rush of warmth and anticipation.

And the reason for it all? Mr. Wylie Anderson. The thought of him, the bond we've started to build, the hitch he puts in my step when I think about being close to him—especially hanging out my bedroom window, gagged by his fingers as I tried to hold back moans while he pounded me.

I can't help but smile as I go about my day, lost in this new glow. It's like I'm walking in a soft bubble of happiness, suspended in the promise of what could be. Maybe, just maybe, I can take care of everyone on the ranch and be cared for in return.

"Boone. Boone Earl Adams."

The sound of Beau's voice, so similar to my own, washes

over me, not quite registering as I stare, lost in the mixer blades whirling in the bowl.

"Oh, hey." I turn the mixer off, taking a swipe of the whipped cream.

"What are you daydreaming about?" Beau walks next to me, staring at me with his head cocked. I nod at the bowl, and he shakes his head, steals a taste, and pops his finger in his mouth.

"Delicious," he says. "As usual."

"Can't have waffles without whipped cream." I lift the beaters and unlatch the bowl from the stand.

"Technically, you can." He wipes his finger on his shirt. "But I'm sure glad we don't."

I smile, floating over to the cupboard and grabbing the large mint serving bowl.

"You sure seem smitten lately." Beau leans against the counter, arms crossed.

I raise my eyebrows and curl half my mouth up.

"Yeah, I've noticed." He swipes another taste. "So has everyone on the ranch. Just wanna make sure you're… okay."

Beau knows me better than anyone. Ma said when we were learning to talk, we'd babble, talking in incoherent sounds, having complete conversations only the two of us seemed to understand.

"I'm fine." He reaches for another sample, and I smack his hand away.

He huffs a breath, a sound I'm well-versed in.

"I'm fine." I repeat, and move to him, grasping onto his shoulders, peering into eyes that reflect my own.

"Okay, okay. Listen, I'm your big brother. It's my duty to worry about you."

"Nothing to worry about," I say, pulling him into a quick hug.

"You know these cowboys." He draws back, returning to lean on the counter as I plug the waffle iron in. "Just passin' through. A different conquest at each stop. I want to make sure you take care of... this." He walks over and pokes my chest.

"Cowboys, eh? Takes one to know one, I guess." I give him a teasing smile.

"Exactly why I'm worried."

"Well, don't be." I pop the bowl of whipped cream into the fridge. "And you've stayed."

"'Cause I have reason to." He wraps his arm around my shoulder. "A few, actually."

"Well, maybe Mr. Anderson does, too."

"Sure hope so." Beau gives me a peck on the cheek, the smell of his tobacco deodorant mixing with the cinnamon in the waffle mix.

"Now, make yourself useful and take those out." I nod toward plates of eggs, bacon, and biscuits. "Winnie's off, and these waffles won't make themselves."

"Sure thing."

Beau picks up a few platters before he pauses, and says, "Love you more than corn in the fields."

"Love you more than stars in the sky." I return my half of the mantra we've shared since forever.

My twin brother, my steadfast protector—of my body, soul, and heart—heads to the dining room, and I get to finishing breakfast.

ONCE I'VE CLEANED up and have lunch prepped and spread out on the buffet, I decide to surprise Wylie with cake. It baked while I was making the sandwiches, and delivering it to him seems like the perfect excuse to steal a kiss in the middle of the day.

Heading out past the barn, I spot him walking with Noodles. He's got the horse on a shorter lead and Wylie's face is focused and calm. His red and brown flannel sleeves are rolled up as the late April sun warms the day. The top buttons are open, letting his chest hair peek out. The memory of burying my face in it sends my heart knocking in my chest.

There's a quiet ease to their stride, the kind that comes with familiarity and trust. In only a few weeks, they've built a partnership nobody expected. Wylie walks beside Noodles, the horse's strong, steady steps matching his own. His hand rests lightly on Noodles' neck, and there's a softness in the way he touches the horse. My heart melts witnessing their connection.

But just as I'm about to approach, something catches my eye. I glance over at the barn, and sure enough, there's Dennis poking his head out from behind the door. His ears flick back and forth like he's got a plan brewing. And, knowing Dennis, it's probably not a good one.

I watch as he suddenly trots out into the yard, his tiny hooves making a cheerful clip-clop sound on the gravel. Without hesitation, he makes a beeline for the paddock—for Noodles—his little tail flicking like a mischievous spark.

Dennis loves to stir up a bit of chaos, and it's clear that today is no different. He lowers himself close to the ground, and more like a cat than a horse, manages to scoot under the fence. With a playful nudge, he nips at Noodles' flank, causing the larger horse to snort in surprise and shuffle away a few steps. Noodles doesn't seem particularly bothered, though—like the other animals, he's already used to Dennis' antics.

Wylie lets out a chuckle, shaking his head as he watches the mini horse bounce around in the most dramatic way possible. Dennis gives a little hop, a snort of his own, and then races around Noodles in a wild circle.

"Dennis, you rascal," Wylie mutters with a smile, clearly amused by the playful antics. He shakes his head again, but there's a warmth in his voice that tells me he's not really mad.

Watching Dennis run circles around Noodles while Wylie calmly walks alongside brings a wide smile to my face. The contrast between the two horses couldn't be more obvious—Noodles is all solid, graceful strength, while Dennis is a whirlwind of mischief and speed. They're like night and day, but somehow, they make a perfect pair—kind of like Wylie and me.

As I walk closer, a flutter reverberates through my chest. There's something about the way Wylie interacts with the animals, the easy care he shows them, that tugs at something deep inside me. It reminds me of Pa and my siblings. I've always had a soft spot for cooking, but connecting with animals never came as naturally to me, and I deeply admire those who have an innate way with them.

I lift the cake in my hands, a small offering to add to the moment, and take a step forward.

"Hey, there," Wylie says, draping the lead around Noodle's neck.

He walks over to the fence, and to my surprise, the horse follows even though he's now free to roam.

"Brought something to add to your little party."

"Dennis wasn't invited, but..." he looks at the tiny

bugger trotting around the perimeter, seemingly making his own fun.

"He has a way of inviting himself," I say.

"Exactly."

Dennis arrives near us, pauses, and shakes his head furiously until Wylie reaches down and gives his mane a pet.

"You little stinker," he says.

Dennis takes this as his cue to jet off.

Noodles pokes his nose at Wylie's shoulder, and he wraps his arm around the horse's head, gently petting the soft skin below his eye.

"Think he'll be ready to participate next weekend?" I ask.

"Walking with me? Probably. But he's not ready to let me mount him. We'll have to work up to it."

"Relatable."

Wylie laughs, his cheeks tingeing red and making my pulse pick up.

"Who'd have thought he'd be so tame," I say, handing the cake over to him. "Before you arrived, we'd all but given up on him."

"Just needed something to sweeten the deal." He nods to the cake. "And the right person, I suppose." He turns and kisses Noodles right on his nose. The horse nudges into him, and my insides roll like Ma's old wooden pin over freshly made dough.

Wylie gazes at me, his eyes locking with mine. There's a depth in his stare. Sure, he's talking about Noodles, but maybe, just maybe, he also means us.

18
———

## WYLIE

WITH A SIGH, I kick off my boots and stretch out on Boone's bed. I might like fucking with 'em on for a spell, but keeping them on too long isn't comfortable or clean. My toes need to breathe.

Boone's cuddled up to my chest, doing his best to be the smaller one, even though he's not. The room smells like sweat, leather, and cum. Why someone hasn't bottled that up as a cologne yet is beyond me. It would fly off the shelves faster than a stallion at full gallop.

"Mmmh." Boone moans into my skin, his sweet breath making the hair on my chest flutter.

"Okay if I stay?" I ask.

I've spent the night in his room a few times but don't want to assume. We barely fit on Boone's double bed, but we'd fall off of my single like a couple of ol' coyotes at the edge of a dry creek—hanging on by a whisker.

He nods into me then reaches up, kissing on my neck. The smell of me is all over him, sending a shockwave to my cock and leaving me wondering if I could get it up for round two so soon after finishing.

142

Boone's naked body is pressed up on me. Skin to skin. Yeah, I've messed around with guys over the years, but it was never like this. Stayin' after. So much kissin'. Snuggled up like two bugs in a rug.

I squeeze his torso, pulling him tight, wanting him closer.

"You okay?" His voice comes out tired and hoarse.

Probably from moaning into my fingers while I attempted to split him open like a stubborn leather hide.

"Oh, yeah."

The words come out, but the tremble in my voice betrays me. Maybe he'll just think I'm spent.

Boone props himself up on his elbow, eyeing me like I told him the sun was gonna rise in the west.

"What is it?" He lays his chin on my chest, staring up at me with those green eyes, and I take a breath.

Boone's words echo in my head. *You're safe.*

"Just, strange. Feeling like I could stay. Not movin' on."

"Did you talk to Beau?"

"Soon. Told him I need to chat. He gave me a slight smile and a short nod. Thinking he's probably on to me."

"Yeah, probably." Boone kisses my chest, right near my heart. "But that's good. It'll make things easier."

"That's what I figure."

"So what do you feel off about? Having second thoughts about staying?"

"No, that's not it. Just... not used to this," I say, struggling to find the right words. Boone burrows into me, and I squeeze him tight, inhaling his slightly sweet scent. "Being comfortable."

"Is it your family?" His eyes blink up at me, and I try to focus on 'em. "You never talk about them."

I pull my lips in, closing my eyes. If I'm staying here on

the ranch, with Boone and his family, he needs to know. Keeping it in won't help anything.

My eyes open to his handsome face, grounding me to the moment.

"Grew up in central Wyoming. My folks were kind. Loving. I had two younger brothers, Luke and Jesse. I was the oldest, though there was only about a year and a few months between each of us. We worked hard, played hard. It was a good life, mostly. Until it wasn't."

Boone brushes some hair from my damp forehead. A refreshing breeze blows in from outside, but between the rustling we did before and now thinking about my family, I'm sweating like a whore in church.

"What happened?"

I reach for his face. He's so damn beautiful. That dimple catches my thumb, and I close my eyes, letting it all spill out.

"It was a bitter winter's night. Smelled like snow but the forecast didn't call for it. Well, that storm rolled in faster than anyone could have predicted. I was out on my horse checking the herds, when Jesse came shouting from the truck. Pop had collapsed after putting the last of the cattle in the barn. My brothers tried to get help, but the storm was too fierce, and by the time the doctor made it out, it was too late."

"Oh, Wylie, I'm so sorry."

I rub my thumb across his face, the soft indentation making my heart so damn happy. It's a small, almost imperceptible detail, a tiny feature maybe only I notice, a private treasure just for me. The way it deepens when he smiles, or the way it's there even when he's lost in thought. I wonder if he even knows how much that dimple tethers me.

"Heart attack. It was rough. Sudden. As bad as losing

Pop was, it only got worse. My brothers and I drifted apart. Luke turned to the bottle. He was so angry all the time. Jesse pulled away too. Burying himself in the work of the ranch, trying to do it all. I did my darnedest to hold us together, but it seemed like the tighter I grasped, the more they slipped through my fingers."

Boone's eyes are fixed on me, unwavering, as if he's trying to read every thought running through my mind. I'm not entirely sure, but it looks like there's a shimmer in the corners of his eyes. I'm not trying to upset him, but there's no way around it. If he wants me sticking around, he has to hear it—needs to know what I'm carrying, even if it's hard to say out loud.

"Didn't think things could get worse. Fuck, I wish I was right about that. Luke's drinking escalated. Seemed like he'd wake up and start. Driving an hour to the closest dive bar. Not coming home until it was almost time to get up and get to work. When he didn't come home one night, I knew something was wrong. Jesse and I searched for him for days. Maw was a wreck. It wasn't until the snow melted a week later that we found him..." My voice breaks, but I force it out. "Frozen, alone. Gone."

Boone doesn't speak. He pushes himself up, nuzzling into my neck, kissing the top of my shoulder, holding on to me like he knows I need an anchor—his breath warm and steady against my skin. The weight of his arms envelops me, and for a brief moment, I wonder if he fears what the truth might do to us.

"That broke me. Pop. Luke. My family, the only thing that ever really mattered, was gone. I couldn't stay on that land anymore—couldn't breathe the same air. The memories... the guilt... I couldn't save them."

"Wylie."

"I know. It's not my fault. I've heard it before. Don't know what else I could've done. I tried my hardest, but I couldn't hold us together."

He's kissing my face now. My cheek. The corner of my mouth. His arm, lassoed around me, pulls me close. I try to swallow, but it's hard moving anything past the lump in my throat.

"So, I left. Ran away. Didn't even say goodbye to Maw or Jesse. My heart still aches about that. Packed my bag and walked off into the horizon. Been too embarrassed to even call, let alone visit. But maybe someday."

I let out a deep sigh, releasing some of the weight that's been pressing down on me for so long.

"Been working ever since. Hitchin' between jobs. A month here. Two there. Never overstaying my welcome. Searching for something—anything—that might give me a moment's peace. But even with the miles between me and the pain, I never could find it."

My fingers move to Boone's chin, pulling his face to mine. Making sure he sees me when I say it.

"Till you."

He's quiet for a moment, his gaze steady, like he's chewing over everything I just said. Without a word, he leans in, his lips brushing mine with a slow, deliberate kiss. It's a promise, raw and unspoken, as if to say that as long as we've got each other, nothing else matters. In that moment, it settles deep down in my bones—the kind of certainty only a man like him can offer, as sure as the sun setting over the horizon.

## 19

## BOONE

WITH BREAKFAST over and the kitchen tidy, I set about slicing the ham to make sandwiches for lunch. The knife moves easily through the tender meat, and I place each piece carefully on a plate, savoring the quiet rhythm of the task. With the back door open, the last of the cool morning air sighs softly through the screen, carrying the sweet, earthy smell of damp grass. As the sun climbs higher, its warmth creeps in like a promise of the day ahead.

I hear Billie before I see her, rustling out back with the hose. Probably rinsing off her tools or not wanting to use a glass, taking a quick drink.

"Abilene Anne," I holler.

She doesn't say a word, just steps inside, wiping her mouth with the back of her arm before walking over and lifting her chin. I take the hint and lean down to kiss her cheek. Little sisters really are a gift—one of those quiet blessings that only us with 'em can truly appreciate.

"Didn't mean to interrupt." She nods to the knife in my hand.

"Never bothering me," I say. "What's up?"

She situates herself on the stool, curling a leg up, wrapping her arms around it, showcasing her ink.

"Taking a break. Told Winnie and Pepper I'd show them how to use the new stencil machine before I haul it to the studio. Just needed a breather first. Ham smells mighty fine."

"Brown sugar. Ginger. Figured I'd get it sliced before it gets too hot out."

She nods, her eyes flicking to the knife in my hand. "Beautiful out now, though."

I shrug, though I'm already thinking about how much of the day is slipping by. "Yeah, hoping to get outside this afternoon." I don't need to say more. Billie knows me about as well as Beau. "But you didn't come in to talk about ham or the weather, did you?"

She meets my eyes, the air between us shifting just a little. "Not exactly," she says, drawing out the words. "Was actually wondering about you and Wylie."

I pause, the knife still in my hand, but I don't move it. "What about us?"

Billie tilts her head, studying me like she used to do to the poor frogs she'd catch by the creek. "I don't know. You don't seem to talk much about your... situation." She raises an eyebrow. "What's going on?"

I blink, not sure if I'm relieved or uncomfortable. "Why the sudden interest?" I ask, though it comes out a little more defensive than I mean to be.

She shrugs, one side of her mouth curling up in that half smile of hers. "Just curious. You seem... happy. Happier than I've seen you in a long time."

A grin seems to arrive out of nowhere on my face. The thought of him. Us. Knowing my family's noticing.

Billie taps her finger lightly against her toned arm, eyes

glinting as she lowers her gaze for a second. "I mean, do you think it's... gonna work? Between you two? He mentioned taking off after the rodeo."

Saturday—only a few days away. Wylie still hasn't talked to Beau. After all we've done. All he's said. My gut tells me he wants to stay, but 'course it's possible he's having second thoughts.

I take a deep breath, unsure how much to say. Billie's always been sharp, and there's something about the way she asks that makes me want to be honest. Plus, I've never been able to fib to her.

"It's complicated. We've got this... connection. On the one hand, it's amazing. Wonderful." I scrub my face, the stubble coarse. "But I'm also scared. Of letting him in. Of him leaving."

Billie's quiet for a long moment, the weight of my words hanging in the air. Then she looks up at me, eyes soft but steady. "Nobody's saying you've gotta figure it all out right now. You do so much caretaking. And we all appreciate it. You. Love you. But, Boonie, maybe stop trying so hard to carry it all on your own. You're allowed to be taken care of, too. People—especially the ones who love you—are supposed to help with that."

I blink at her, surprised by the insight. It's not what I expected, but it's exactly what I needed.

"Yeah," I say, offering her a slice of ham, "maybe you're right."

She gives a little nod, as if that's all she wanted to hear. Then, without missing a beat, she grins. "But hey, whatever you do, don't forget to save me one of those sandwiches. This ham is freakin' delicious."

I chuckle, nodding my head. "Now, that I can do."

THE REST of the day passes quickly, a blur of busy tasks and familiar routines. Pris helps me prep the chickens out back for the barbeque, her sharp knife skills making quick work of the butchering while I season the meat, a mix of salt, pepper, and Ma's secret spice blend. The smell of the marinade fills the air, mingling with the earthy scent of the ranch.

When we finally sit down to eat, Ma's sauce receives the usual round of praise—everyone's favorite part of the meal, always. Even though I've seen it a hundred times, there's something about the way the sauce glistens on the grilled chicken, the tang of tomatoes mixed with the smoky sweetness of the grill that makes it irresistible. A warm smile bubbles on my face when I imagine Ma giving an approving nod up in Heaven.

After dinner, Winnie, always the organized one, takes over with a quiet determination, finishing up the dishes and prepping for breakfast. It's almost like clockwork, the way she moves—efficient, careful, never rushing but always getting things done. I give her a minute to finish up, making sure the kitchen is tidy before I turn toward the back door.

Cool evening air arrives just as the sun dips lower in the sky. It's time to clean the grill. The barbeque still holds the remnants of a good meal, the charred bits of chicken skin and the faint smell of smoke lingering. I grab the wire brush, the scraping sound against the grill's surface oddly soothing, almost meditative. As I work, my mind wanders, the quiet of the evening settling over me like a blanket.

I know Wylie wants to stay. Not because he's said it, which he has, but because it's the kind of thing you pick up on, like when you can tell a dish is just about ready without even looking at the clock. It's a feeling, deep in your gut.

I've stopped asking about talking to Beau. Don't want to pressure him. He's got to do it on his own. Pa used to always say, "A man's got to find his own way, even if it means stumbling through the dark to get there." Some things, you let unfold in their own time, like Noodles learning to trust Wylie—it takes patience.

Once the grill's clean, I sit on the two hay bales gathered out back for that purpose, watching the sky turn darker and the stars blink into existence. I don't rush back inside. A chill settles in, and for a second, everything slows down, the rhythm of the day fading into the calm of the evening.

"Best damn barbeque I've ever had."

Wylie's voice comes through the screen door.

I don't reply right away. The wooden frame slaps softly, like he held it until the last moment. Dried straw shifts under us as he takes a seat next to me.

"Glad you enjoyed it," I say.

"Still got a taste of it on my lips. Kinda hope it lingers for a spell."

I raise an eyebrow. "Mr. Anderson, are you hinting at something?"

I turn fully toward him, the moonlight catching the angles of his face, all stubble and jawlines. His eyes widen, and his brow lifts, as if I've just asked him if he's seen a pig flying across the sky.

A playful glint sparkles in his eyes. "I realize it's your family's recipe, but..." He taps a teasing finger near his lips. "Wanna taste?"

I can't help myself. His charm, his mouth, the way he's looking at me—he's impossible to resist. Without thinking, I lean in.

For a moment, I'm stuck there, caught in his gaze, the pull of something I can't quite define tugging at my torso, like he's daring me to take the bait.

I slope forward just a little, drawn in by that quiet confidence he wears so effortlessly. I'm close enough now to feel the warmth of his breath, to see the way his lips curl ever so slightly at the corners, taunting me.

He doesn't move, doesn't push me. But there's a stillness in the air between us. It's charged with the kind of tension I can't ignore.

"You're trouble, you know that?" His smile widens, eyes glinting. "The best kind."

And for some ridiculous reason, I can't argue with that.

My mouth lands on his, and before I get to kissing him, I run my tongue along his lips, and sure enough, there's a hint of sauce there. Mostly ginger and cumin, and a satisfied grin eases onto my face, thinking about him savoring it as I do the same to him.

"Mmmh," he moans into me. "Nothing compares to these."

He takes a nibble at my lower lip, sending sparks through me—just a gentle, teasing tug, but enough to make everything else fade into the background. The light pressure of his teeth against my skin sends goosebumps rushing over my arms.

For a moment, there's nothing but the soft brush of his lips and the lingering warmth of his breath. His eyes are steady on mine, and there's something unspoken between us. This isn't like anything I've experienced before. Pretty sure it's love.

I can feel the pulse in my neck, the quiet thrum of anticipation as his tongue parts my lips. Carefully, he pushes me against the house, moving an arm across my chest, holding me in place. He's so close, and yet my mind wanders away. I don't mean to, but a sound escapes my mouth into him. A whimper, like a hurt animal.

Wylie pulls back, scanning my face, as he pushes his hat back into place.

"Did I hurt ya?"

"No, I'm good." I tug on his shirt, wanting him near, but also scared of what that means.

He moves forward, taking my gesture as an invitation to return, but I move my face to his shoulder, looking up at him.

"No, Boone. You're not okay. What's going on?"

He bites at his lower lip, moving his hands to my waist, never breaking contact.

"Rodeo's Saturday."

"Reckon Noodles isn't ready to ride," Wylie says, face softening as he talks about the horse. "But I can walk him, show him. Dennis will tag along to soothe him from the crowd. It'll be good for him. Noodles, not Dennis. That bugger's got more confidence than a bull in a china shop."

"Can't wait to see it," I say.

His firm chest under my cheek, looking away, feeling brave, I spit it out.

"And then, thinking about where you'll go next?"

"'Scuse me?"

He pushes me off him, sitting up straight, taking my hands in his.

"Boone Adams. You listen to me." His thumb and index finger grasp my chin, drawing my gaze to his. "I'm staying. Thought you wanted that." He runs his thumb along the back of my palm. "Been spending all my nights in your room, anyway. Hoping to make it permanent if you wanted. Would free up my room for someone new."

My heart picks up, hearing him say it.

"But you haven't..." I pull my lips in, my head shifting, taking another route. "Want me to talk to Beau about it? About you. Staying. Really, I don't mind."

"Already asked him to chat tomorrow. I need to do this. 'Cause it's not just about me staying."

His fingers land on my face, his thumb sweeping across my cheek.

"Huh?"

My mind races, trying to figure out what he's talking about.

"Boone, I want you to be my buckaroo. My cookie. My guy. This is all I want." With his free hand, he pats my chest, right where my heart beats. "You. I finally feel at home. And well, with your folks gone, gotta talk to someone about my intentions. Seems Beau fits the bill."

My whole body buzzes. Like spurs stirring over my skin —from the tips of my fingers to the deepest part of my chest. The world seems to shift, and for the first time, maybe ever, everything feels... right.

Leaning into his touch, I lift my chin, capturing his lips with mine, kissing him like our futures depend on it— because, after what he's said, it sure seems like they do.

## 20

───────

## WYLIE

AFTER I'VE FED and watered the horses, I move on to checking their stalls. I carefully remove the manure and toss out any damp bedding, making sure the space is clean and dry.

Dennis, the little rascal, follows along, his tiny hooves clomping on the floor as he trails me from stall to stall. It's like he's supervising my work, keeping a watchful eye on every move I make—but also pushing his nose at me, hoping for a scratch under his chin. His loyalty is unwavering, and though he's small, he's got the air of a big-time barn manager.

With everyone fed and settled, I grab the grooming brush. The bristles are well-worn, but they've worked their magic on countless horses. I make my way over to Noodles, who's already standing by his stall door, ears flicking back and forth as he watches me approach. After a few weeks of this routine, he knows what's coming. His soft, bay coat shines in the dim light of the barn, and I spot a few stray bits of hay stuck in his mane.

He gives a soft nicker to greet me. As I begin to work the

155

brush through his coat, he angles into my hand, content and relaxed. The rhythmic motion of the brush helps me settle into a peaceful routine, accompanied by the soft swish of the bristles and his occasional snort as he shifts his weight. It's a moment of quiet connection between us, a time to check in before we head out to the paddock.

Boots echo through the barn, growing louder as they approach, and I swallow hard. I've been avoiding this conversation for a while, not because I don't want to stay, but because I'm not sure I'm ready to lay it all out there. Asking for more work, explaining what's going on with Boone and me, not wanting to leave—it's a lot to say. But if I want to stay on—be here, with Noodles, with Boone—then I can't keep dodging it. The time to speak, open myself up, has come, ready or not.

"He's lookin' fine." Beau stands outside the stall, leaning on the door. "You've been real good for him."

My lungs fill with a satisfied breath, knowing he's talking about the horse, but offering a silent prayer for the same sentiment about his brother.

It's a funny thing, being with someone who's got an identical twin. At first, they're hard to tell apart, but the more time I spend with Boone, the more it's clear—they're not as alike as they seem. It's like the differences in their personalities have bled into how I see them.

"Just needed the right person." My eyebrows gather as a small knot forms in my stomach. "Not saying y'all aren't— it's just, well, sometimes..."

My words get stuck in my throat, heat rising at my collar. For fuck's sake, I'm messing things up before I'm even able to bring up Boone.

"Chemistry." Beau lifts his hand, palm up, offering an apple, and Noodles, tentatively sniffs, his lips curling around the skin before chomping into it. "You and him have it."

He pats Noodles' head. "Good boy." The horse doesn't move away or flinch. "Looks like he might participate Saturday. Reckon he's not ready to ride, but think you could show him?"

"For sure. On a lead. Maybe if I persuade him with the right food."

"There's no pressure. Two years and he hasn't participated, but obviously we'd love to include him. He's a handsome boy."

Dennis trots over, enters the stall, and weaves between Noodle's legs.

"Yes, Dennis. You're still the most handsome." Beau gives the little bugger's chin a quick scratch. "These two have really hit it off. Dennis never took much of an interest before you arrived."

"I think he realized I needed help."

"Well, Dennis is your man. Or horse, I suppose. He's got a knack for taking charge."

He kneels down and gives Dennis a hearty pat on the flank, prompting the horse to whinny and trot out of the stall, heading outside to make mischief.

"Off to make sure someone else is doing their job," he says.

He stands, leaning against the partition separating Noodles from the next stall.

"Listen, we've enjoyed having you around. Boone especially." He catches my eye and there's a knowing look there. "After the rodeo..."

A sudden fluttering, like a trapped bird, takes over my chest. I take a deep breath to steady myself.

"About that." I pause the brush on Noodles, but keep

my hand on his back, the rhythmic beat of his heart beneath my hand.

Beau doesn't budge. He's crossed his arms, waiting patiently for me to spit it out.

"I'd like to stay. If there's room. I mean work. Happy to keep spending time with this guy." I run my fingers through his mane, the soft hair slightly wavy from brushing. "And the other horses. Anything you need really. Just ready to… ya know…"

"Put some roots down." He walks over and places a hand on my shoulder.

"Yeah."

"Be happy to have you." His fingers grip my shoulder, giving it a good squeeze.

I nod. A new sensation coming over me—reckon it's belonging.

"As for my room," I say, keeping my gaze on the horse. "If you need it, I'll be out on Saturday."

"Pardon? You just said…" His eyes narrow, and his mouth hangs open as it clicks into place. "Oh. Oh!"

"Boone's invited me to stay with him." Even though Beau's clearly figured it out, I need to say it. "And I want you to know, I'm telling you this because I care about your brother. A lot. More than I've cared for anyone. I know it's only been a few weeks, but… he's special to me."

Beau looks at me with eyes so similar, yet so different, than Boone's.

"We've got something. Never thought this would happen for me. But something about this place. The people. Your brother."

I pause, trying to find the right way to explain—how unexpected it is, how right it feels, even though it came out of nowhere.

"It's like... I didn't even realize how much I was missing until I got here. I don't think I even knew what I needed. But Boone—he's different. Not just the way he looks at me, but the way he *sees* me. I didn't expect it. Never thought I was the kind of man who could... fall for someone like this. But with him, it's just right."

I glance at Beau, whose face has softened, but there's a flicker of something—maybe surprise, maybe something else —still there.

"I don't want you to think that I'm rushing this or that it's just some impulse. I care about Boone, and I think he cares about me too. And I want you to know that, in case there's any confusion."

I let out a slow breath, hoping my words are making sense. The air between us feels heavy, but I need to show this isn't about anything sneaky or hidden. This is me, opening up, hoping he understands this isn't some fling.

He watches me for a long moment, his lips pressing together, as if weighing everything I've said. Noodles' skin twitches under the brush where I've paused, and I resume grooming him.

Finally, Beau nods slowly.

"I get it," he says, voice quiet but steady. "Just... take care of him. He's my brother. My other half. Don't need to say much more than that."

And in that moment, I know it's not about the words. It's about the trust. Beau's letting me know, in his own way, that he understands—Boone and I need a chance, and my staying is the only way to make that happen.

I nod. "Of course. You have my word."

Beau taps my chest lightly, then gives a playful punch, his smile spreading wide. Unlike Boone, there's no dimple to soften the grin, but if there were, it would be right there, on full display.

A deep sense of peace settles over me—my body calms—knowing this is precisely where I'm supposed to be.

Beau catches my gaze, his shoulders back as his mouth cracks into a grin.

"Mr. Anderson. Welcome to Rainbow Ranch."

## 21

## BOONE

MY BODY STIRS and half an eye opens to pitch darkness. As the person in charge of breakfast on a working ranch, my body has adjusted to waking before the sun and rooster, but lately, it's been harder to get out of bed. Each night after cleaning up from dinner and doing whatever prep is needed for the next day, he's there. On the stool or outside the back door on the hay bales. Waiting for me.

Last night was no different. When I didn't spot Wylie in the kitchen, I took two sweet teas out back, and sure enough, he was leaned against the house, feet up, shirt open, exposing his tank, with a long piece of hay between his teeth, making my insides simmer.

Without talking, he sprung up, taking a tea from me, and we headed off to walk the back roads of the ranch—which meant strolling along, stargazing, while Wylie snuck kisses. And I, having no willpower against him, played right along.

After a quick walk past the barn on our way back to check on the horses, we ended up where we always do, in my room. It's only been a little over a week, but the familiarity of having him next to me, his smell—like earth and sagebrush mixing with our sweat and semen—lulls me to sleep like a baby. Each morning I deliver a soft kiss, doing my best not to wake him before I pull on my clothes and head down to the kitchen.

With the rodeo only a day away, I've been juggling my regular work all week with preparing the carnival-style food for our guests. It's a lot of work, but Pris, Winnie, and Pepper help, and it's a great way to make some extra income for the ranch.

With a deep inhale, taking it all in and thanking the heavens for the blessing, I roll over to give Wylie his morning peck on the cheek. But he's not here.

Not in bed.

Not in the room.

I click on the small lamp on my bedside table, eyes squinting at the blast of light, trying to see some sign of him, but there's nothing. Taking my clothes from last night from the chair, I get dressed and head downstairs. He's probably with Noodles. With the rodeo looming, I'm sure Wylie wants to check in. He has every morning all week. But not until I'm up.

Doing my best to keep my boots quiet, I head out to the barn. It's still dark, and the animals aren't really up. There's no sign of Wylie. As I walk down the aisle, the horses stir slightly. Dennis blows a burst of air out of his tiny nostrils. Usually, I'd stop to give him some attention, but not this morning. I walk past him to Noodles' stall. Empty.

My heart bursts into a full gallop in my chest as I head out to the smaller barn. The truck and horse trailer are gone.

I head back to the house, less worried about making noise, and up to my brother's room.

"Beau, Beau."

We don't typically go into each other's rooms unannounced, and certainly never without knocking, but Beau and I shared a room until we were almost sixteen. I've seen and heard it all.

He's dead asleep. Mouth hanging open, breathing heavily.

I poke at his naked shoulder, not too hard, but I need him to wake up.

"Wha—? What's wrong?" he grumbles.

I take a seat as he rolls over, covering his face with his forearm.

"It's Wylie. He's gone."

He smacks his lips and moves his arm just enough for an eye to peek out.

"Maybe he took a walk. Did you check the barn?"

"Yeah, Noodles is gone."

"Well, maybe he finally mounted him." His voice still sounds gravely. "Or took him for a walk."

"Truck's gone. Trailer too."

This gets his attention. He moves his arm, sits up, giving me a look that says *oh fuck*. Growing up, we got in our share of mischief, and I know it well.

"And he didn't say anything to you?"

I shake my head, tears stinging the corners of my eyes. Wylie admired the truck so much, but he wouldn't steal it. My head gets all woozy, and I'm glad to be seated on the bed.

"Did he leave anything? A note?"

I open my mouth to reply, but it's drier than the fields after a drought. Nothing comes out.

Beau moves to the edge of the bed, grabs his jeans from

the chair that matches the one in my room, and pulls them on.

"Come on." He wraps his arm around my shoulder.

Having Beau with me instantly begins to settle my nerves. He has always taken care of me, not just with his actions but with the quiet strength in his eyes that lets me know I'm never alone. When it felt like our world was falling apart after our folks died, Beau was the strong one—holding everything together on the ranch, offering a stability that kept us from completely unraveling.

He'll know what to do. He always does.

"Let's see what we can figure out," he says, hooking his arm in mine and leading me downstairs.

Beau's office illuminates when he clicks on the small antique lamp on the corner of his desk. He opens the laptop. Besides our landline, with no cell service out here, it's our primary connection to the rest of the world. Fingers fly on the keyboard, and I stand behind him, trying to figure out what he's doing.

A map appears. There are dots, some are moving, some aren't.

"Where's that?" I ask.

"Rainbow Ranch. These dots are all the animals." He points to a tiny blue dot erratically moving back and forth. "Pretty sure that's Dennis."

He shrugs, then continues searching the map.

"All the animals get microchipped and have GPS devices on their breakaway halters. Helps if anyone gets loose." He swallows hard. "Or stolen."

My heart sinks. Wylie wouldn't do this. Take Noodles, the truck, and the trailer? Bolt off without telling me? He wants to stay. Sure, people say things they don't mean, but it wasn't just his words. It's the way he holds me. Stares into my eyes. Grasps my face when we kiss. It doesn't add up.

"Noodles definitely isn't on the ranch," Beau says.

He's moving the mouse, the map expanding on the screen, when the sharp, jarring ring of the house phone blasts through the quiet, making us both jump like jackrabbits.

Beau snatches the receiver, and even in the pre-breakfast quiet on the ranch, I can't decipher the voice on the other end. After a moment, Beau speaks.

"Doc Evans..."

The vet in Johnson Springs. My stomach flips.

"Thank you for calling... Yeah, I know..." He runs his fingers through his hair, tugging at the back like he does when he's thinking. "Okay... You sure you don't want me to come? Got it." Beau's head nods repeatedly. "Thanks again, Doc. He does? Oh, sure."

Focused on the call, he musters up a faint smile, but then catches my gaze and gives me a wink.

That one gesture hits me like a splash of cool water, washing away the tension and leaving me with a deep sense of relief. There's more talking on the other end, more nodding from Beau and finally, he speaks.

"Will do. Thank you, Wylie."

Beau hangs up the phone and takes a deep inhale, closing his laptop and sinking back into his chair.

I draw a slow, cleansing breath, feeling the tension in my shoulders ease slightly, before he speaks.

"Wylie took Noodles to Doc Evans. Apparently, when he went to check on him this morning, he was lying down in his stall, awake, biting at his stomach." He rolls his shoulders back, sitting up a little. "Most likely colic. Doc thinks it might be from too many sweets. Something about cake..."

My heart rattles around my chest. *Oops.* "Sounds like Wylie caught it just in time. Doc is giving Noodles fluids and watching him for a few hours, but if all goes well, they should be back by this afternoon.

"Wylie did the right thing. Gonna cost a pretty penny, but with Doc's discount, it shouldn't be too bad. Hopefully, we make good money at the rodeo to offset it." He rubs his chin. "Said he didn't have time to leave you a note but thought you'd look in your closet."

My stomach flips and my mouth opens, but nothing comes out. I'm too busy bolting out of Beau's office like a pot on the stove about to boil over.

In a flash, I'm up the stairs and in my room, my heart pounding in my chest. The closet door is cracked open a few inches, but I didn't notice when I rushed out to the barn. I swing it wide, and sure enough, hanging there on the hook is Wylie's weathered hat. The sight of it hits me like a punch to the gut—because it's not just his hat, it's a piece of him.

He's staying.

---

## 22

# WYLIE

ON SATURDAY MORNING, Boone is up even earlier than usual for rodeo prep. Last night, laying on my chest, he went on and on about mixing the menu up each month depending on what the ranch produces. Of course, folks like what they like, and you can't get too fancy if you want to make money.

He showed me his menu, scribbled out on a notepad he keeps next to the bed. Besides the funnel cakes, corn dogs, and roasted corn on the cob they always serve, this month Boone wrangled up a BBQ brisket chili and jalapeno cornbread. My mouth watered as he explained each dish, and when he heard my stomach growl, he crawled up for a kiss.

I grab my hat from the hook in the closet and head out to check on Noodles. As of last night, he was in good shape. Doc Evans flushed him out something good. Poor guy had a tube shoved up his nose into his stomach for a few hours, but after some blood tests, Doc gave me the all clear to bring him home.

Home to Rainbow Ranch. Somehow, both Noodles and

I found our way to this place. I don't know if it was fate or a twist of luck that led us both here, but here we are.

The first time I laid eyes on him, I knew he was something special. He has the kind of presence that charges the air around him. I remember the way he looked at me when I stepped into the barn that first day—curious but cautious. He was scoping me out.

I arrived here a mess, no better than a weather vane caught in a windstorm, blown about by poor decisions and regrets. But something about this place spoke to me. The animals. The land. The people. Boone.

Rainbow Ranch has a way of pulling folks—and animals—in, giving them a place when they've got nowhere else to go. I'm sure grateful Noodles and I ended up here at the same time. The bond between us is new, fragile, like two wild creatures who've just found shelter from a storm. But I can already feel it. It's as if the earth under our feet has whispered that we belong to each other now.

Last night, Noodles sure seemed ready to be shown, but Beau and I agreed it might not be best to push him. I'd love to walk him around the ring on a lead. Introduce him to the world. Let everyone see how far he's come. But I'm letting Noodles decide—we can always try next month. Or the month after that. Neither one of us is going anywhere.

On rodeo day, breakfast consists of pre-made egg sandwiches left out for us, so I sneak out back to steal a kiss from Boone. He's wiping out the cotton candy machine, and I come up behind him, wrapping my arms around his waist.

"I thought you weren't keen on sweets," he says, running a cloth along the glass.

"Only if it's your sugar." I kiss his neck and push myself into him. "Fuck, you drive me wild."

He spins me around and kisses me, and in that moment,

with Boone and a future together solidified, all the tension that held me down seems to evaporate. A lightness I've yet to experience comes trotting in. Damn, it feels good.

"Okay, cowboy. I need to get this ready to churn out clouds of fluff for the kids. I'll see you soon."

I nod, dipping back in for one more kiss from my guy before heading back to the barn.

When I arrive, Dennis has managed to let himself out. He's waiting by Noodles' stall, kicking at the ground until I open it and let him in. With the medication Doc Evans sent us home with, Noodles seems more and more like himself every hour, and there's a noticeable spark in his eyes having his little buddy weaving between his legs.

I touch his nose, giving a soft pat before running my palm along his face and down his neck.

"Whaddya think, boy? Ready to meet the world?"

He nestles into my shoulder, and my arm instinctively wraps around his head. This is how we hug. If he were able, I like to think he'd crawl into my lap like a dog.

"We'll take it easy. I promise. We'll be right with you," I say, brushing away a piece of hay from his face.

Dennis lifts his head, poking at my waist, and I reach down and give him a scratch.

"Okay, guys. Let's show 'em how incredible you are."

---

THE AIR HANGS thick with the scent of leather and hay, mixing with the faint, sharp tang of livestock. A patchwork of sunburned faces and faded denim fills the bleachers, all eyes fixed on the arena. In the center, a cloud of dust rises as Beau, Billie, and Benny enter the ring. Colorful rainbow flags flap in the breeze as hooves pound the earth. The low murmur of excited voices hums under the harsh twang of Winnie's fiddle. The announcer's voice crackles over the loudspeaker, blending with the distant whinny of a horse. The heat of the sun beats down from a cloudless sky, as the rhythmic pulse of the rodeo begins to take shape—a symphony of dust, grit, and raw energy.

I'm standing by the center entrance, off to the side, waiting with Noodles. He was calm as I attached the lead to his halter, but Dennis, who's less keen on being tethered, is growing impatient with his. I plan to release him as soon as the arena clears, but if I let him loose here, he'd bolt.

The Adams siblings ride out, tipping their hats at me, and I give Noodles a quick pat on his side. I'll participate in some of the later events without Noodles.

The announcer's voice booms over the crowd. "Everyone, everybody, while we wait for the next round of barrel racers, we have a special treat for you."

I lean into Noodles, resting my head near his ear and whisper, "Let's go, boy. I'll be right with you."

Holding each horse's lead in a different hand, we head into the ring. With the gate closed, I unlatch Dennis, and he immediately takes off, trotting around the edge, taking short leaps, showing off. Lord, he's a ham.

Noodles stands still, his body slightly stiff as he eyes the lead rope in my hand. His ears flick back and forth, processing the unfamiliar pressure of having a sea of eyes on him. When I give a gentle tug, he takes half a step forward. I rest my hand on his shoulder, applying light pressure.

"You got this, boy."

My mind races, torn between holding steady and turning around and heading out. But as if he senses something's off, Dennis comes around the corner, stopping beside Noodles. He nudges the larger horse's front leg, and

Noodles shifts his weight ever so slightly. With a quiet stir, Noodles moves forward, Dennis leading the way, their hooves making a soft, steady clop on the dirt.

Quiet, measured clapping comes from the onlookers, and Noodles lifts his head a little, picking up his pace to a slow trot to keep up with his tiny leader. His ears flicker, and when the applause from the crowd picks up, he lets out the cutest little snort. I jog alongside him, head held high, the sun beating down on my hat.

Out of the corner of my eye, I catch sight of Boone off to the side, leaning against the entrance. He's grinning wide, his face catching the light, somehow making him even more handsome. I keep pace with Noodles, taking in the crowd as Noodles makes his rodeo debut.

After I get Noodles settled in his stall, I've got a bit of time before the modified roping exhibition, so I head over to the food stalls by the barn. Tables stretch down the side of the building, smoke rising from grills, huge pots bubbling, and trays piled high with breads and sweets. At the far end, I spot Winnie working the cotton candy machine, the pink and blue sugar spinning into fluffy clouds on paper cones for the crowd.

I finally spot Boone again, ladling out chili into bowls for a long line of folks waiting their turn. Pris and Pepper are on either side of him, helping. Slipping behind the table, I sidle up beside him, not making a sound.

"Need any help?"

"Hey, you." He flashes that grin of his, and for a moment, it feels like the whole damn world could be saved with that smile. "Aren't you busy?"

"Got a few minutes..."

He places the bowl on the table next to a row of others, and seizing the moment, I gently knock his hip with mine.

"Pris, I'll be back in five," he says.

She's placing slices of cornbread on the edge of each bowl.

"Got it, boss."

Pepper takes over ladling the smoky chili into bowls, and right there, in front of all those people, Boone takes my hand, interlacing our fingers, and tugs me off, around back, and inside the barn.

It's warmer inside and filled with the soft scent of hay and dirt. Sunlight filters through the small windows, casting a golden glow across the exposed wooden beams overhead. Boone pushes me against hay bales stacked in the corner, a few pieces of hay crunching under our boots.

With his body pressed against me, he leans in, and before I can speak, his lips are on mine—strong, forceful, like he's been waiting all day for this. I kiss him back, slow and sure, the distant hum of the rodeo outside wrapping around us. Boone's heartbeat hammers against my chest.

"You were amazing out there," he says, pulling back.

I shrug. "It was all Dennis, really."

He kisses me again—shorter, sharper this time—and the intensity of the moment leaves me breathless.

"Really glad I'm staying," I say.

He buries his face in my neck. We're both sweaty, ripe from the day, but it doesn't matter.

"Cookie, can you look at me?" My voice comes out barely more than a whisper as I tip back just enough to see Boone's big green eyes. "Please."

He shifts his weight, his gaze locking with mine. I cup his face in my hands, my thumb tracing the curve of his dimple, the warmth of his skin grounding me in a way nothing else can.

"I love you." The words, a quiet confession, slip from

my mouth like a sigh of relief, the weight of years of searching and unspoken feelings finally released. With a soft smile, I pull off my hat and settle it onto his head. "Cowboy."

He laughs, low and rich, before dragging me close, kissing me like he means it with every ounce of his being. When he pulls back, his breath warm against my lips, Boone Adams says, "I love you, too."

The words settle deep in my chest, right where they belong.

I'm finally home.

THE END

# EPILOGUE
## BOONE

Three Months Later

THE SADDLE FEELS like a giant fist around my ribs, and every step the horse takes sends a jolt up my spine. I grip the reins tighter, though I'm not sure it actually helps. My legs are still too stiff, my feet not quite settled in the stirrups, and I can't stop glancing at the ground beneath us—the dirt and rocks that seem so much further than they ever did on foot.

"Remember, Cookie. Relax," Wylie calls from ahead, his voice easy, like he was born in a saddle. He's barely even looking back, just trotting along, Noodles moving like he's done this a thousand times.

I force a deep breath. Relax. Right. Easier said than done when you've never ridden more than a handful of times and now you're miles from home on a trail with nothing but wide open spaces and the sound of hooves.

"Yeah, I'm good," I say, trying to sound casual, but I know my voice—a little too tight—betrays me.

Wylie convinced me to ride. Or try. Benny was in on it, too. Even Sassafras, the chestnut mare whom both my brother and boyfriend deemed docile enough for an inexperienced rider like me, seems unsure about my declaration of being okay. She flicks her ears back toward me like she's aware of my thoughts.

Does she know I'm not confident? Does she care? I push that thought away as the wind picks up and the trees thin out, opening into a vast stretch of meadow. Noodles moves ahead like he's eager for the open space, but Sassafras... she just keeps plodding along at her own pace, steady and unbothered.

"You okay back there?" Wylie glances over his shoulder now, raising an eyebrow.

"Yeah. Fine." I try to smile, but it's more of a grimace.

For a second, I wonder if I could slide off and walk instead. A day trip to explore. That's all Wylie wanted. No, me riding on Noodles with him wouldn't be safe. For us or the horse. Yes, he'd be right there with me. I'd be safe as beans in a pot on this gentle horse. She wouldn't swat at a fly with her tail.

Sassafras snorts, like she can read my mind.

"Remember, darlin'," Wylie calls over his shoulder. "Just trust your horse."

Trust my horse? The thing I'm pretty sure could buck me off without breaking a sweat?

"How far are we going again?" I ask, anything to distract myself from the sensation of my body swaying with every step the horse takes.

Wylie shrugs, looking at the path ahead. "Couple miles, tops. You'll be fine. Once you get the hang of it, you won't even notice."

I try to believe him. But as the trail dips and the horse

moves under me again, I can't help but cling a little tighter to the reins. Maybe I'll just take it one step at a time. One jolt at a time.

After even more ups and downs in the terrain, I slowly acclimate. There's a gentle energy to Sassafras—when she's not flicking her ears at me. I take deep breaths, like Billie told me, and maybe, just maybe, the horse senses my nerves calming.

"Almost there." Wylie turns over his shoulder and shoots me a wink.

And damn, if the sight of him with jeans stretched as he straddles the saddle doesn't flood my basement. It's been over three months since Wylie moved into my room. He didn't have more than the clothes in his bag, but I cleaned out two drawers in my dresser for him. Least I could do for the guy that stole my whole damn heart.

I always thought, especially after Ma and Pa passed, it would just be me taking care of my siblings and the ranch family. Never minded it either, but now, with Wylie, I see there's more. So much more.

My eyes trip between Noodles' ass and Wylie's, remembering what Beau told me. *Watch the ass in front of you.* Pretty sure he meant only the equine ass, but here we are.

As we come over a small hill, I glance up, a giant oak tree even bigger than the one on the ranch comes into view. Wylie makes a noise, something between a click and a cluck, then squeezes his legs, making Noodles gallop over to the trunk. With a tug at the reins, he turns the animal, and they're facing me.

Sunlight cascades between the branches and lights them, Wylie's face shaded by the wide brim of his hat, and for a second, I forget to breathe. Not only does he look like the epitome of a Hollywood cowboy—rugged, handsome, a slight sweetness to the way his lips curl up in a way only I'd notice—but he's waiting for me. Me.

"Come on, cowboy," he yells.

I don't make any noises with my mouth or apply any pressure to the horse's sides under me. But Sassafras keeps walking in the slow methodical way she's done the entire trip until we approach Wylie and Noodles.

"Takin' your sweet time?"

I smile. It's genuine, but with a little push, I make it even bigger.

"We're in no rush, right girl?" I pat Sassafras' neck and she lets out a soft nicker.

In one fell swoop, Wylie hops off and, while still holding onto the reins of his own horse, takes mine. He grabs a long rope from his waist and ties it around the trunk using some intricate knot I've seen my siblings use. With a click, he attaches two ends of the rope to both horses' halters in another knot.

"Damn, sure are good with those hands," I tease from my perch.

Wylie's eyes linger on me for a second before he goes back to securing the horses.

His reply is to take my hand.

As our skin makes contact, a wave of relief washes over me, the underlying stress that plagued me throughout the trip out here melting away like ice cubes left out in the sun. Even up here on this horse, with the earth a little too far away for my liking, he's got me.

With a deep breath, I carefully remove my feet from the stirrups, swing my leg over the horse's back, and, with Wylie's steady hand guiding me, slide down, the horse's warmth fading as I land softly in the best possible place on the planet—right in Wylie's arms.

"There's my guy," he says.

When he draws me into his arms, the entire ride out here fades away. His warm body against mine, smelling like leather and hay, envelops me. He holds me close, always tight enough to make us both feel safe. I rest my head on his shoulder, the steady rhythm of his heartbeat soothes me. Wylie Anderson, the quiet, hardened cowboy who walked onto Rainbow Ranch a few months ago has become the piece of my puzzle I never knew was missing.

"Now, I'm starving." His lips are close enough for me to nibble, and I take the chance for a quick kiss.

"Are you?" I ask.

Wylie's stomach growls like a trapped bear, and a laugh barrels up from my chest and flies out of my mouth.

"Told ya," he says.

He removes my hat, placing it on the cantle of the saddle, and takes hold of my face. His lips are soft—thanks to the eucalyptus balm I gave him—as he applies gentle pressure. My heart flutters as he deepens the kiss. We've both got the rest of the day off, so there's no rush. Winnie will serve the chili mac casserole with a green salad and fresh bread we prepared this morning. I melt into Wylie's kiss, closing my eyes, allowing the rest of my senses to cherish this delicate, perfect moment.

His stomach gurgles again, and I giggle into his mouth.

"Okay, okay," I say, pulling away. "Let's get you fed, cowboy."

With the picnic items we packed in Noodles' saddlebags, Wylie spreads the blanket under the tree while I unpack the food.

"We've got shaved turkey sandwiches, corn salad, and of course, some cake." I hand him a bottle of sweet tea, imagining the lingering flavor on his lips when I kiss him later.

Noodles lets out a sharp nicker, and we both turn toward him.

"Sir," Wylie snaps. "No cake for you."

Beneath the cool shade of the tree, we stretch out on the soft, well-worn blanket, savoring our lunch. The air is warm but gentle, a perfect harmony of sun and breeze, as the day unfolds beautifully around us.

"Thinking I might bring Jesse out here in November."

I check Wylie's face, and there's no sign of unease. A couple of months ago, he mentioned reaching out to his mother, and I was, of course, supportive. Beau gave us the office phone while he was out working, and I sat in the chair across from the desk. He's called twice more since then, and now his mom and brother are planning to drive out for Thanksgiving.

"Bet he'd love it." Noticing he's finished the salad on his plate, I dish out a little more. "And your mom can show me this famous caramel brownie recipe I keep hearing about."

Wylie smiles—slow, warm, and completely unguarded, like the sun breaking through clouds after a storm. His eyes light up, sparkling with an affection so pure that it seems as if he's looking straight into my soul. The slight crinkle at the corners of his eyes and the tenderness in the curve of his mouth—every part of him seems to express a quiet adoration, utterly devoted and unspoken.

"Finally, I can get some good grub out here," he teases.

"Excuse me?"

"Look at me, Cookie." He puts his plate down and raises his flannel, revealing his gorgeous stomach. "I'm wasting away to nothing."

"Oh, really?" I run my hands over his exposed skin, the light dusting of hair taunting my fingers. "I can think of a few things to feed you."

"C'mere." Wylie's voice is quiet but commanding, and before I can even respond, his hands grasp me. His arms slide around my waist, tugging me forward, pulling me off balance as he shifts beneath me. There's a sharp intake of breath as I land on top of him, the weight of his chest pressing up against mine. He falls back with a soft thud, his body relaxing into the movement, and I'm caught in the gentle curve of his hold.

"Boone Adams, I love you."

Before I can respond, his lips find mine—filling me with every ounce of emotion. I hold him close, embracing him in a way that I hope assures him he's safe. He pulls back, and I plant a kiss on the side of his face as I lean my head next to his. My lips land near his ear, which I also kiss, before whispering, "I love you, too."

He holds me tight, and lying here under this giant tree with Wylie Anderson, it's never been more clear. We've got each other. Here. Now. Always.

# WANT A SNEAK PEEK OF BEAU'S STORY?

First Chapter of Lasso Lovebirds by Clio Evans...

## BEAU

In my experience, things have always happened in threes. As my boot squelched into a third pile of horse shit this morning, I had to wonder if the universe was just pokin' fun at me. A curse wrenched from my lips, and I glanced around out of habit for any of the teens on our ranch—even though I was most assuredly alone.

If one of them caught wind of me cursing, I'd never hear the end of it. The good news was that the sun had barely risen, and while I wasn't the only one up this early, I *was* the only one trudging through a field to fix a fence's wiring before the rain hit.

"Damn it," I muttered, kicking my heel out.

Shit plopped into the wet mud, the ground damp from the constant storms we'd had over the last couple weeks. Thunder rumbled in the distance as I crossed from the stables to the parked truck. I got in, shutting the door quietly and cranking the engine.

I hoped I could knock this out quickly to make it back in time for breakfast. Otherwise there'd be hell to pay from my twin brother, Boone.

Of the four of us, Boone was the only sibling that could wrangle me indoors. Maybe it was the sticky buns or maybe it was the fact that we'd shared the same womb, but he always managed to *know* when something was off with me. Just how I knew the same about him. It was a sixth sense. Which was why I needed to fix my attitude—and clean off my boots real good—this morning before walking through the dining room door.

As the eldest, the weight of running the ranch and always having the right answers sat on my broad, sun-tanned shoulders. I rarely got a moment alone, which was why I often jumped on tasks like this. Mending a fence before dawn meant I could have a little time to myself to ponder, dream, and spiral.

What was putting my hackles up this morning wasn't the fact that I'd just stepped into a pile of shit. And it wasn't because of the storm brewing just a few miles north, or even the usual pressure of being the boss.

It was something else entirely.

I turned on the radio as I rumbled down the dirt road, using the few minutes of peace to think.

Ever since Boone and Wylie had fallen for each other, I'd been painfully reminded of the fact that I was alone. And it was silly, right? I was so damn happy for the two of them, that it hurt. Hell, we all were. They were perfect for each other. Billie, our younger sister, and Benny—the youngest of the four of us—thought so too.

Romance was in the air. And while it was beautiful and

heart-warming, it reminded me of the secrets I'd been keeping. It reminded me of the deep pining I had for someone I *couldn't* have, and how I'd probably end up growing old alone.

Rainbow Ranch was the love of my life, right? That had to be enough to fill the cavern that echoed in my chest.

My headlights beamed through the grape-crushed dawn as I slowed to a stop, spotting the marker I'd placed the other day to show where the fencing needed repair. I turned off the truck and hopped out.

I tightened my tool belt as I trudged over to the fence. This patch-up was right near the front gate, which was exactly why I'd wanted it done so fast. I couldn't have our fences looking rundown, especially where it was visible from the paved road.

Three flags billowed as the wind whipped up—a brilliant rainbow, a bright pink, blue, and white, and our symbol: a horseshoe with two R's and a rainbow connecting them, representing Rainbow Ranch. I scowled, slamming my hand down on top of my cowboy hat before it was blown straight off by the breeze.

"Damn," I muttered, my brows shooting up.

I came prepared with my fence stretcher, fencing sleeves, pliers, and a set of gloves. But as I started to pull on the gloves, the wind slammed into me again, this time whisking my hat straight off my head and tumbling into the field.

"Damn it!" I yelled, stumbling forth to catch it before it went to our neighbor's property.

This time, the thunder sent a chill up my spine. I glanced up as another set of headlights blinked on the paved road. A raindrop hit my forehead right as a white truck with what appeared to be saucers—*are those satellites?*—on top.

The tires skidded to a halt in front of the gate. I stared as the last of the sunrise was clipped by dark, roiling clouds. My eyes widened as I realized a wall was forming in the sky. The wind became more violent, the flags thrashing relentlessly.

Someone short with bright green hair hopped out of the vehicle, waving their hands wildly. They pointed to the sky, and my stomach dropped as the clouds began to swirl in a way I knew all too well.

Living in Oklahoma, tornadoes weren't all that rare. But one forming right here on the ranch? I couldn't remember the last time that'd happened.

"Do you need help?" I shouted, already rushing toward the gate.

"Can I drive in?" they yelled back. "It's coming in fast!"

My chest constricted and I nodded, unlatching it quickly. The metal groaned as I fought to pull it open, my heart beating so loud I could hear it over the violent storm. I watched the stranger get back into their van. They floored the gas, launching over the cattle gate and onto our graveled road.

They rolled down the window. "Get in," they shouted.

*Gosh, they're pretty to look at.* I swallowed hard and pointed at my truck. "Follow me to the ranch."

When I looked back up at the sky, my stomach twisted —a funnel was starting to form. I needed to get back to the house. Now.

I sprinted to my truck and got into the front seat, slamming the door shut. The tires peeled over the gravel as large raindrops pelted the windshield, the wind rocking the cabin as I turned to speed back toward the ranch. I checked the rearview to make sure the stranger was following behind me, and they were.

"Fuck," I growled as the funnel reached for the ground behind us.

It was gonna land. Now the question was whether or not it'd follow us.

It'd been a long time since we'd had a storm season quite like this, and the thought of Rainbow Ranch being swept away by a tornado was a worry I had every year. Everything could be gone in the blink of an eye, and then what? What would I do? What would we do?

I wasn't religious. Never had been, never would be. But still, I sent up a silent prayer, a wish, a hope—whatever it was. I just wanted them all to be safe. My family. The ranch. The animals.

The truck jerked. My knuckles whitened as I gripped the steering wheel, my boot pushing the pedal into the floorboard.

Even going this fast, it'd take a few more minutes to get back to the house. The funnel looked like it'd touched the ground, tearing up the earth behind us. My heart rumbled, fear streaking through me.

"Please go," I whispered. "Please let up."

My throat was dry. Every muscle was tense enough that I knew I'd hurt tomorrow.

I could see the stables in the distance. My eyes darted from what was in front of me to the horror behind me—and then I blew out a breath in relief.

The funnel was going a different way. I slowed down, the adrenaline making me tremble as I pulled to a stop on the road, the stranger stopping behind me.

"Fuck. Shit. Damn it. What the fuck?!" I needed to get all the curses out while I could.

I kicked open the door and got out of the pickup, my knees feeling like Boone's strawberry jelly. The stranger hopped out too, raking their fingers through their green hair.

I approached them, a lump forming in my throat. "Well, that was one way to meet someone," I said. "I'm Beau Adams."

They held out a hand. "Sky Williams." They turned their head to look at the retreating clouds, their expression turning wistful. "Wish I could have grabbed a few pictures of that one. Glad it went the other way though, otherwise we would have been sitting ducks. I take it this is Rainbow Ranch?"

The corner of my mouth tugged as I shook their hand. Their skin was smooth against my calluses. "What gave it away?"

Sky grinned. "Well, for starters, you're the only ranch I've seen in hours with the pride flag and trans flag at the gate. Plus, I've heard of this place."

I raised a brow. "Are you looking for a place to stay?"

"Well," they hesitated. "Maybe? Johnson Springs didn't exactly feel like the friendliest place for a nonbinary person. Not that anywhere in this state really is..."

"You'll be safe here," I promised.

Sky cleared their throat, their pretty brown eyes dropping down. I realized I was still holding their hand. Their cheeks flushed as I released them, taking a step back.

"Sorry," I added. "I think I'm a little scatterbrained from the storm." What the hell was this heat creeping up the back of my neck?

"That was a close call," they agreed.

"How about you come in for breakfast with everyone and we can talk afterward?" I asked. "Could use some food after that scare. My brother makes the best breakfast in the state."

Sky smiled, dimples pressing into their apple cheeks. "Bold claim."

"Well," I chuckled. "I'll let you be the judge of that. Welcome to Rainbow Ranch, Sky."

Continue reading Lasso Lovebirds now!

# ACKNOWLEDGMENTS

I want to tip my (imaginary) cowboy hat and express my deepest gratitude to my fellow ranchers: Clio Evans, Ashley Bennett, and Max Walker. Thank you for wrangling me into Rainbow Ranch and making my first shared-world writing adventure an absolute delight. I'll never stop yelling from the rooftops—or the barn loft—about how extraordinary you all are.

As a gay city boy with zero horse sense, I leaned heavily on the equine expertise of others. Kayla Grosse (and Atlas), Jay Leigh, and Jennifer Marcom—thank you for your wisdom, help, and saint-like patience. Noodles, Dennis, and I owe you our eternal gratitude.

And to my husband: thank you for tolerating my sudden cowboy era, complete with yee-haws, flannel, and questionable cowboy purchases. You're the real MVP (Most Valuable Partner) and my forever buckaroo.

# ABOUT THE AUTHOR

M.A. Wardell lives near the ocean with his husband and cats. When he isn't writing, he's snuggling those cats, reading all the rom-coms, walking to unravel plot points, and taking long hot baths. He loves playing matchmaker on the page and has many more stories planned.

For more information, visit https://www.mawardell.com/

Purchase signed copies here!

For access to exclusive content and merchandise, join me on Patreon.

# ALSO BY M.A. WARDELL

## **THE TEACHERS IN LOVE SERIES**

*Teacher of the Year* - Marvin and Olan's story is available now!

*Mistletoe & Mishigas* - Sheldon and Theo's story is available now!

*Napkins and Other Distractions* - Vincent and Kent's story is available now!

*Husband of the Year* - Marvin and Olan's series finale coming November 2025

## **BIG BOYS SMALL SPACES SERIES**

*Marshmallow Mountain* by A.J. Truman and M.A. Wardell - Data and Marsh's story out now

Cut to the Feeling by A.J. Truman and M.A. Wardell - Bryce and Emerson's story Coming September 2025

Download free bonus stories!

https://www.mawardell.com/freebies

www.ingramcontent.com/pod-product-compliance
Lightning Source LLC
Chambersburg PA
CBHW031045310726
48969CB00007B/2120